PRAISE FOR

A PLANET FOR RENT

"Yoss' smart and entertaining novel tackles themes like prostitu-
tion, immigration and political corruption. Ultimately, it serves
as an empathetic yet impassioned metaphor for modern-day
Cuba, where the struggle for power has complicated every facet
of society."

JUAN VIDAL, NPR, BEST BOOKS OF 2015

"In prose that is direct, sarcastic, sexual and often violent, *A
Planet for Rent* criticizes Cuban reality in thinly veiled terms.
Cuban defectors leave the country not on rafts but on 'unlawful
space launches'; prostitutes are 'social workers'; foreigners are
'xenoids'; and Cuba is a 'planet whose inhabitants have stopped
believing in the future.' The book is particularly critical of the
government-run tourism industry of the '90s, which welcomed
and protected tourists—often at the expense of Cubans—and
whose legacy can still be felt today."

JONATHAN WOLFE, *THE NEW YORK TIMES*

"Some of the best sci-fi written anywhere since the 1970s. . . .
A Planet for Rent, like its author, a bandana-wearing, muscly
roquero, is completely sui generis: riotously funny, scathing,
perceptive, and yet also heart-wrenchingly compassionate. . . .
Instantly appealing."

ANDRÉ NAFFIS-SAHELY, *THE NATION*

CONDOMNAUTS

ALSO BY YOSS

A Planet for Rent
Super Extra Grande

YOSS

CONDOMNAUTS

Translated from the Spanish by
David Frye

RESTLESS BOOKS
BROOKLYN, NEW YORK

First published as *Condonautas* by Casa Editora, Havana 2013

This work is published with the support of Charles Dee Mitchell.

First Restless Books paperback edition July 2018

ISBN: 9781632061867
Library of Congress Control Number: 2017963941

Cover design by Edel Rodriguez
Set in Garibaldi by Tetragon, London

Printed in Canada

1 3 5 7 9 10 8 6 4 2

Restless Books, Inc.
232 3rd Street, Suite A111
Brooklyn, NY 11215

restlessbooks.org
publisher@restlessbooks.org

For Susana and Roland,
because this idea for a possible story
came up on their visit to Havana,
and now it is a novel.

For Elizabeth, my little muse.

CONDOMNAUTS

THE SKYSCAPE SPLAYED ACROSS the holoscreens turns from pitch black to navy blue to baby blue to milky white. I glance at the instruments and punch in a landing course correction. The numbers on the altimeter fall precipitously, and at last the dense ammonia clouds open up to give me a view of the ground below.

Right on target. It would have been easier to let the satellite feedback positioning system take over, but I like to pilot old-school: one man with his skill and intuition, controlling a machine with its sensors and thrusters. And thanks, but no AIs.

Flying solo like this is one of the special perks I get now and then on my job as a Contact Specialist, or "condomnaut," as we're usually called. Social relations—playing well with others—was never my strong point, and on a small hyperjump frigate like the *Antoni Gaudí* you don't exactly get a lot of me time.

My little two-seater traces an elegant curve, coming in low to cruise over the desolate gray basalt landscape of Discovery Valley. Slowly, steadily, I drop speed on the approach and at last bring the shuttle to a smooth stop with millimetric precision, level with the ground, a prudent five hundred meters from the Alien vessel. Even at this distance, though, I'm entirely in its shade.

"Good job, Dralgol." I whisper my congratulations to the thrumming shuttle, enjoying my privacy and keeping the helmet mic flicked off as long as possible.

The antigrav launch is the smallest of four shuttles we keep on our Catalan frigate. Its official name is the *Drag d'Algol*, but I prefer my nickname for it, Dralgol. It's a comfortable but sporty little speedster, perfect for planetary scouting, even a short orbital trip. I like to use it when I'm going to make Contact, while letting the frigate hang back prudently in orbit. The ship wouldn't have any problem landing—its 1,200-meter hull is aerodynamically streamlined—but best not to risk our only ticket off this forsaken planet.

Like the rest of the crew, I've examined the Alien ship from every angle our teleguided holocameras could record over the three days of inactive waiting prescribed by the Protocol for First Contact. But even so, I have to say: it's very impressive from up close.

Not because it has a strange profile or an unusual design. Just the opposite. Its design is perfectly ordinary for an inter-stellar vehicle, human or otherwise: perfectly spherical, matte surface. But what floors me is its size. The only word I can think of is: gigantic.

It doesn't look like a vehicle created by sentient creatures so much as a part of the natural rock-strewn, canyon-laced land-scape where it has come to rest. Like some enormous metallic carbuncle that has come to fill the floor of a valley as inhospitable as the rest of the planet's red topography.

Space is full of the weirdest formations, after all. I've seen things that most geologists only dream of—or have nightmares about. Planetologists, I mean. It's hard to avoid being anthropocentric, even now.

But the thing is, it isn't really sitting on the valley floor.

It's hovering just above it.

And if there's one thing you'll never see a natural magma extrusion do, it's break the universal law of gravity. In Rubble City we had a saying: If it's green like a guanabana, and sweet like a guanabana, and prickly like a guanabana, it's a guanabana. Not that any of us had ever seen a real guanabana fruit, except on commercials, much less eaten one.

So, it's artificial.

And as soon as I admit this to myself, some odd mental calculus automatically makes it look even bigger.

Not even the Qhigarians' ramshackle worldships are anywhere near as big as this. Not to mention, spherical shapes aren't exactly a Qhigarian thing. As far as I know, no explorers from the Nu Barsa habitat (or any other human, I'd bet my hide) has ever come across a race in all their travels that constructs spaceships as huge as this.

Also huge: our stroke of luck when we saw it in motion. If we'd only seen it sitting here, still as a rock, like it is now, we'd probably have taken it for a natural feature of the valley.

That's how enormous it is.

The next big thing may be whatever comes now, on this remote planet in Radian 1234, Quadrant 31.

It's funny how the ancients, as sharp as they were about some matters, believed blindly that their convoluted historical star charts, with their constellations and their ecliptics and their Arabic names for stars, would be around forever. It never occurred to them that the arrangement of the night sky that their astronomers were familiar with only made sense when you viewed space from the vantage point of Earth. Of course, those ancient astronomers never imagined the Galactic Community.

Paradoxically, a few Alien races prefer our allegory-rich human names for them. Such as the Algolese, the race from the fifth planet around the great star Algol in Perseus. Now, that may be because their real name is unpronounceable—unless you use ultrasounds in your everyday speech, that is. Likewise, the Arctians, the natives of the ninth world orbiting the red giant Arcturus in the constellation Boötes, gladly adopted the semi-affectionate shortened form of the name that our old poetic Earthly system assigned them, because it had never before occurred to them that their race needed any sort of distinguishing name at all. They had always been just plain "us"!

There are more things in heaven and earth, Horatio . . .

For example: this planet, which we've even gone to the trouble of officially naming Hopeful Encounter, orbits a red star in the northern hemisphere that's concealed from view on Earth, as it turns out, behind bright Vega.

Until yesterday it was just like a trillion other planets in the galaxy: completely unknown to Earth's ancient astronomers. And moreover—according to the restless Qhigarians who were the first to map this sector of the galaxy (and so many others), many centuries ago—absolutely unfit for supporting oxygen-based life forms. One more ball of stone, one of a gazillion desolate naked rockscapes. No dangerous chemicals to worry about, for sure, but no water or interesting minerals, either. So not only had it never been explored by human ships, it wasn't likely to get explored anytime soon.

Well, nobody said everything in space had to be interesting.

And it probably would have stayed on that list for thousands of years, if sheer luck hadn't intervened.

Hell of a drug, luck.

Even after our umpteenth hyperspace jump on this trade exploration journey left us right on the edge of the system's gravitational sphere of influence, given that it had no resources we'd be interested in—no radioactive elements, rare metals, water, or free oxygen showing up on the spectra of any of its eight planets—we most likely wouldn't have even bothered to stow our six jump antennas.

We would've just used the gravity of the system's primary to recharge our gravitic batteries for the next hyperjump. And then—see ya later, system.

I've often thought that having a simple way to travel faster than the speed of light has done more to hamper than to facilitate the detailed exploration of the trillions of worlds in the galaxy. It's like trying to learn about every nook and cranny in a territory by flying over it in a supersonic plane.

The hyperengine we all use—Qhigarians, humans, Algolese, Furasgans, Arctians, basically all the thousands of races that now make up the Galactic Community—is an ancient Taraplin design. That mythical species, whose name in their own (lamentably forgotten) tongue meant "Wise Creators," disappeared from the galaxy so many eons ago that not even their faithful heirs, the Qhigarians (which means "Unworthy Pupils," of course) remember what they looked like.

Nor is there any clear explanation for why or how the alleged Taraplins disappeared—though many Qhigarians believe (or pretend they believe; never can tell with those crooks) that over the course of the millennia their beloved teachers accumulated so much power and wisdom that they simply transcended their mere physical state and became gods.

Luckily, before they Transcended, or died out, or disappeared, the Taraplins were generous and far-sighted enough to bequeath to their protégés, the Qhigarians, a stock of a few quadrillion engines, in three sizes or classes.

The hyperjump procedure is as simple as can be. All you have to do is set the coordinates for your destination and make sure that the entire hull of your ship is inside an imaginary polyhedron (specifically, an octahedron with eight identical triangular sides) drawn from the endpoints of the six long, thin antennas, which you must fully deploy in order to generate the field. When the antennas are energized, a microsingularity is generated in the space between them on which surrounding space tends to converge; but hyperspace cannot be squeezed flat, so the ship has no choice but to pop out of our three-dimensional space into an equidistant hyperspace—from which, when the energy impulse is turned off, it emerges once more into the regular cosmos, like no big deal. But suddenly you're many lightyears away.

Simple, right? In practice, at least. Yes, the Taraplins were geniuses.

In fact, to the mortification of millions of human and Alien brainiacs, nobody's been able to figure out the specific physical principle behind the ancient and incredibly effective devices that allow us to maintain faster-than-light travel across the galaxy. Try to open one and it dissolves in seconds, as if eaten by some powerful acid.

So we're forced to buy each and every one of our hyperengines from the Taraplins' savvy heirs, the Qhigarians, who are the only ones who know how to activate them. Though to be fair, they sell them and turn them on for an astoundingly low price, considering how greedy the Unworthy Pupils are in all their other business dealings.

As magical as it is as a transport system, hyperjumping also has its limitations. The most aggravating is that you can hardly ever jump straight to where you want to go. The routes through hyperspace, for reasons that not even the Qhigarians are able (or willing) to explain, appear to shift around all the time. Sometimes the same journey that took you just five jumps of a hundred lightyears apiece in one direction will force you to take six, seven, eight, up to twenty jumps of barely thirty lightyears each on the way back.

The Qhigarians don't try to explain hyperjumping; they just believe in it. And in selling tons of hyperengines. But scientists, whether human or Alien, aren't generally very big in the faith department. That's why there are as many theories about how hyperjumping works as there are races in the Galactic Community.

The Furasgans, for example, believe that the Wise Creators set down a limited number of roads through hyperspace, along which the ships run like trains on rails. Except that these rails are constantly moving and reorganizing. Hmm.

Kigran rorquals maintain that on every hyperjump, the ship and the crew are annihilated, and what returns to our universe is a quantum copy. Yeah, and so?

Some Algolese and human physicists think superstrings are tangled up in the whole affair. Excellent.

Arctians argue that a hyperjump simply leaves the ship in place while the universe moves around it.

Of course, there are those who claim it's a little of both.

While others say they've got it all backward.

But the hypothesis that, for my money, wins the cake for audacity, originality, and paranoia, is the one I heard Jaume Verdaguer, a young Catalan physicist, expounding one afternoon. Supersmart and crazy as a loon, but the sweetest and friendliest guy you'll ever meet. He and I lived together in a blissful romance years ago.

Jaume and a handful of equally young colleagues, unorthodox fans of conspiracy theories all, simply don't believe that any "real" physics are involved in hyperjumping. Using Occam's razor, they came up with the idea that the brilliant, extinct Taraplins never existed. Moreover, they posit that Taraplin hyperengines are a massive con job being pulled by their Unworthy Pupils. Hyperjumping, they think, isn't an intrinsic physical property of space at all, but a mere mental function. Something the Qhigarians themselves are doing, no less! Like an extension of their strange colonial telepathy, which is undeterred by distance.

Therefore, they think, how hard or easy a hyperjump is at any particular moment depends only on how many worldships, full of Qhigarians concentrating their mental powers, there are in that sector of the galaxy at the time. That's also why it's impossible to leap beyond the Milky Way to regions where none of their thousands of worldships have yet gone.

Personally, I find the idea kind of charming. But as a scientific theory, I'm afraid it'll never be very popular. Believing it would mean, to start with, granting the nomadic, pacifist Qhigarians nearly limitless intelligence and mental power— enough to teleport thousands of ships a second! It's a scary thought.

Besides, if they're such a powerful race, why would they need to keep such a complicated con job going among thousands of races in the Galactic Community?

As it is, hypernavigation is less a science (though that's how the Space Academies teach it) than a sort of intuitive gift, which some people have and some will never learn no matter how hard they try. Like the skill for Contact that we condomnauts have, for example.

Maybe that's why I'm drawn to Gisela, the hypernavigator on the *Antoni Gaudí*. Sheer affinity between two souls who both have valuable and relatively rare talents.

Though hypernavigators are a bit more common, to be honest.

It's platonic between us, of course. With my old trauma, she and I could never . . .

So who cares if she's a skinny freckleface with basically nothing attractive about her, other than an exuberant head of disheveled red hair that cascades almost to her waist. Who cares if she picked that muscle-bound putz Jordi Barceló, the ship's third officer, to be her partner. Jordi, who has an even nastier temper than his cat, Antares. But, man—those muscles.

Better not to think about it right now.

The fact of the matter is, whether it was Gisela's talents or the sheer randomness of galactic routemaking, three days ago we jumped to this unmapped system in Radian 1234, Quadrant 31, almost dead on the galaxy's ecliptic plane, and we would have jumped away almost immediately. Except that Amaya, our methodical sensor technician, glanced at the hypergraph and noticed that something had recently entered the system and hadn't left. Some enormous *something*. Because, as our disconcerted Amaya explained to us, it had to be incredibly huge for her to detect it at such a distance.

As soon as we discovered this monster our priorities naturally changed. Screw recharging the gravitic hyperjump batteries and all the other drudge-work!

This was a really big deal. Maybe even the biggest deal in the past fifty years of human history, the biggest thing since the day when, thanks to Quim Molá's cleverness and lack of scruples, we got those first twenty-five hyperengines from the Qhigarians and reached the stars.

The first reaction on board the *Gaudí* was total celebration. As we had suspected from the beginning, it had to be some sort of Alien spaceship. Then we got scared, just thinking about how powerful its antigrav generators would have to be to lift its massive bulk off the ground. And we scared ourselves even more by trying to picture what sort of beings could build a ship as huge as this—especially since our brilliant Amaya couldn't get her usually superexact biometer to resolve even roughly where they were located inside the immense ship.

In the end, of course, ambition and excitement erased our fears. Nobody had ever heard of such an enormous spherical structure, so maybe we'd hit the jackpot, found what every known intelligent species (a tasteful way to say: any species with commercial ambitions) in the Milky Way, Alien or human, has always been looking for: an extragalactic species. From the Andromeda Galaxy, or the Triangulum Galaxy, or at least one of the Magellanic Clouds.

Our trade opportunities, if we can become the first of the tens of thousands of races in today's Galactic Community to make Contact with beings from beyond the Milky Way—and, by the way, the first to wheedle or purchase the secret to the hyperjump engine that allowed them to cross the currently insuperable chasm between galaxies (and maybe even get our hands on a functional ansible!), putting us on an equal footing to compete with the Qhigarians or even to beat them at their own trade game—would be practically limitless.

Especially for us humans. We're such latecomers to the cosmos that almost every planet in the Milky Way fit for colonization by oxygen-breathing races was already taken by the time we started exploring. The right engine would give us access to practically the entire universe. And with that, we'd come up with not just one, but dozens of worlds that could be turned into New Catalonias, for sure.

Plus, the other races would have to pay us, the way everybody now pays the Unworthy Pupils for Taraplin technology, on which they hold an unbreakable monopoly. And they wouldn't find the new hyperjump drive cheap—we aren't as gullible as the Qhigarians!

It's in this hope that every ship setting out from a human enclave tries to have a Contact Specialist like me on board. Or several, if the shipowner can afford to pay them.

Besides, if they make Contact with some new Alien species on their travels, as happens frequently enough, even with one from our own galaxy, they can let them know that humans come with good intentions. Then they can start off with a relationship of peaceful understanding, trade in goods and technology, as beneficial to both sides as possible—rather than hostile misunderstandings and war, always a bad thing.

Now it's right here in front of me, looming up between the system's reddish sun and myself, its dull shadow spreading across everything as far as I can see.

I've never faced a possible First Contact with extragalactic Aliens before.

What a chance. What a responsibility. I've got equal odds of covering myself in glory or in shit.

Most likely this is just the latest false alarm. But maybe not.

For a long moment I gloat over the thought that these Aliens might really be from beyond the Milky Way. Due to my skills in "sleeping" with Aliens, negotiations with them will be stunningly successful. Nu Barsa will get exclusive rights to the first intergalactic-range (and first non-Taraplin) hyperjump engine in the Human Sphere, indeed in the entire Galactic Community, overcoming once and for all the obstacles to intergalactic travel that have so far prevented us from spreading beyond our own pinwheel of stars.

What will the other members of the union say then? All those snobs in the Department of Contacts who can barely hide their disdain for my not being Catalan and for my "plebe" background?

They'll have to eat their words, en masse.

For example. That stuck-up, envious nanoborg, Jürgen Schmodt. Just hearing that it was me—the immigrant, the plebe, the Third-World condomnaut, the first-generation "natural" talent, the contract worker—and not a member of his team who was lucky enough to make Contact with the first extragalactic Aliens: that will no doubt fry all the high-tech Nazi's nano-circuits, out of sheer spite.

On the other hand, though my obese buddy Narcís Puigcorbé would have happily given his many rolls of fat to be here, I'm sure he'll be glad if it's me, his Cuban *socio*, who wins the lottery.

He's a good friend, the best I've got—maybe because he's ready to retire and he doesn't see me as a threat. If only all the Catalans were like him.

Lovely Nerys, for her part, will also feel proud to the tips of her fins that it was none other than her unmodified first-gen "boyfriend" who took this first step. A small step for me, a giant leap for all mankind. And maybe my self-centered girlfriend will finally give some serious thought to the marriage proposal I made to her six months ago.

That slippery siren is driving me nuts . . .

Apart from prestige, I'll probably also get the Nu Barsa citizenship I want so bad, and with it the security of a steady job. No more freelance contracts. Who knows, I might even stop waking up in the middle of the night drenched in sweat from my recurring nightmare about my disgusting old home sweet home, the Caribbean pigsty of my childhood. City of Havana. Good old CH.

So let me concentrate on my business here. On the here and now, no more distracting memories. Even though I've always found it helpful, centering, to reminisce about stuff that has nothing to do with whatever concrete challenge I'm confronting.

To each his own, you know? Every condomnaut has their own way of making Contact. Some use yoga. Others groove to music. Me, I let my mind ramble while I try to figure out how we got here, humanity and me. Not necessarily in that order.

But. Don't waste your time dreaming about melons when your ass is in the ditch, old Diosdado used to say.

According to our sensors, the local gravity on Hopeful Encounter is slightly greater than Earth's, but still, though we haven't yet managed to catch a glimpse of any of the crew members, judging from the dimensions of their ship and the size of the three or four equally spherical surface vehicles we saw moving around from orbit, it wouldn't be crazy to assume that these presumptive extragalactics are physically much larger than we are.

But will they be slow-moving leviathans with hydrostatic endoskeletons, like the Arctians? Living blobs of undifferentiated cytoplasm, like the Continentines, which I happened to be the first to Contact? Restless, muscular titans that could squash me flat with one false move, like Furasgans when they're still young?

Could be anything. You never know what to expect on First Contact. That's something every condomnaut always does well to bear in mind.

Right now, alone and barely five hundred meters from the mountainous sphere, I'm none too happy at the possibility of getting flattened into two dimensions.

The worst of it is, there's nowhere for me to run if things turn ugly. This dull planet didn't even have the good taste to develop the sort of rough terrain where you might find a cave to hide in. Not even a cleft or two. The rock's too hard. Basalt, is my guess. Not that I'm a planetologist.

I feel like I stick out here like a flea on a shaved dog's bum.

Oh, well. That's how I feel with almost every Contact.

Though this time the danger is a little too overwhelmingly clear.

If I believed in them, I'd be praying to Shangó, Obbatalá, and all the old Afrosyncretic gods of my faraway native Cuba. Praying that these Aliens' idea of a safe distance isn't too different from our own, however huge they may turn out to be.

Instead, I just climb slowly out of the *Drag d'Algol* and start walking forward at an equally measured pace, holding my hands in the air to show I'm not armed.

I'm doing everything to appear friendly and non-threatening, except flashing a smile. Best not to do that.

Though only my remote mission officer can now see my face, hidden under the helmet, the Qhigarians, who know their way around the Alien races of the galaxy better than anyone, always say that we humans are the only known sentient creatures who display our teeth to each other in order to show we are friendly.

Well, I like to comfort myself with the thought that, if the Qhigarians know this about us, why should everyone else know, too? And be tolerant about it.

So, no smiles. The corners of my lips still try to turn up, of their own accord. I must look totally ridiculous. More and more ridiculous by the minute, the more dignified I try to appear.

I move forward in the deliberate, dignified, fearless manner stipulated by the ancient Protocol for First Contact—which was supposedly established by the mythical Taraplins millions of years ago—displaying the absolute calm of a model professional condomnaut. In reality, I feel exposed, vulnerable, even prematurely naked, in spite of my ultraprotect suit.

But at least its triple shielding means that my coworkers from the *Gaudí*, who must be following my every move from the safety of orbit, can't see that I'm sweating buckets and trembling like a leaf in a windstorm. This always happens to me during the preliminary phase of Contact, when I reveal myself for the first time to the Aliens that I'm supposed to make friends with.

Contact Specialist or not, I'm shitting myself with fear. And I don't care.

I was ashamed of these feelings until Narcís confessed to me even he, with hundreds of successful missions on his service record and all the honors a Catalan condomnaut could ever dream of winning, still feels the same pangs in his gut every time he approaches another Alien species.

Nerys also once hinted at something of the sort, in her typically feminine, elliptical way.

I imagine that even pedantic nanoborg, Jürgen, must get some discreet nervous twinges when he makes a new Contact, though I suppose he'd rather be boiled alive than admit it. Stuck-up Prussian.

Yep. Who said that professional daredevils have no fear?

There's a few things I know perfectly well:

That all this is a simple matter of psychology.

That up inside that enormous ship, the Aliens' own condom-naut (or whatever the potential extragalactics call their Contact Specialists, assuming they have such a thing) is most likely feeling at least as scared as I am.

That if I come under attack by disintegrators or hyper-obliteration armaments (if they've got such things and aren't born pacifists like the Qhigarians, who don't dare touch any weapon more sophisticated than a slingshot), the thin mono-molecular ceramic shield of the *Dralgol* won't provide anywhere near as good a defense as my ultraprotect suit.

That if some misunderstanding makes them fire their heavy artillery, the guys on my own ship up in orbit will train all its destructive firepower on the Aliens to avenge me (I want to believe this with all my heart), so there'll be some real hell stirred up right here.

And since nobody who initiates a Contact and has two grams of brains would want to stir up such a disaster, seeing as it would send all their potentially advantageous trade relations down the tubes, the chances of such a catastrophe taking place are slim to none.

But what can I do? I'm sweating and trembling anyway.

Because this could be the one time that the most unlikely possibility comes true, right?

Long ago and far away, when I used to play streetball in Rubble City, CH, with the rest of Diosdado's orphans in El Viejo López's back lot, fearlessly defying the residual radioactivity of the soil, I remember that whenever somebody hit a home run over the fence, one of the older kids would always jokingly say (imitating some old-time announcer, I guess), "And it's going . . . going . . . gone! Adios, my sweet Lolita!"

In this case, it'd be more like, "Adios, Josué!" In other words, much worse. Because, what the hell do I care about Lolita? This is my own life I'm talking about. Okay, true, I risk my life week after week in this funny little business of being a Contact Specialist, which seems the only job I have any talent for. Thing about my life is, I've only got one. And I'm kind of fond of it.

Don't try telling me about the "challenge of the unknown," or my "sense of duty," or how I should feel proud to be in "the human vanguard in the conquest of the Cosmos." Let's be clear: like all my select, envied, and reviled brothers in the trade, I'm in it for the money. Ideals and intellectual gymnastics are fine, but you can't live in the twenty-second century without making a few credits, you know.

Especially not in Nu Barsa, rightly considered the most expensive habitat in the Human Sphere.

So I'm none too fucking relieved to know that, if some paranoid Aliens happened to disintegrate me, the pompous hypocrites would try to wash their hands of it the way they usually do when colleagues die on Contact missions. By slapping my name on some street (not that I'd ever see it) or even on a whole sector of the latest archology.

I'd rather not have any official ceremonies, which my pragmatic Nerys would just exploit to assert her rights as my quasi-widow consort and (most important) as my quasi-heir to grab any bonus pay I might have coming.

So: they can stick all the honor and glory up their . . .

Me being me, I'll take the money and the plaque right now.

But here I am. I've finally come to a complete stop a good hundred meters from the Alien ship.

So I take a deep breath, whisper, "¡Arriba, compatriotas!" like Elpidio Valdés, the hero of comics and cartoons from my Cuban childhood, who rode his inseparable horse Palmiche into battle, wielding his machete to make our island independent from Spain, and—

"Quit dragging your feet, coward."

Damn. I forgot that the mic inside my helmet would automatically reconnect when I left the *Dralgol*. And I especially forgot who'd be listening to me. Wouldn't it have to be Jordi Barceló. And they say there's no such thing as bad luck.

"It's okay if you take your time to make sure they know we have no hostile intentions. But keep walking, fuck it! You've been standing there with your hands in the air for like a whole minute. They're going to think we're vegetables and you've stopped to do some photosynthesizing or put down roots. Come on, Cubanito, shithead, move it or you'll lose your First Contact bonus. And if you make me lose mine, I swear to God I'll cut your servos and make you crawl back to the ship in that lightweight suit of yours."

So charming, so laconic, so homophobic. So tolerant of lower life forms like me, who didn't learn Catalan before we could crawl.

Sometimes I think that if he wasn't the owner of Antares—the lazy, selfish charmer of a ginger cat who's now the whole ship's beloved mascot—I would have tried strangling him long ago.

If none of the other crew members beat me to it, that is.

For instance: Amaya, our sensor tech, who was as taken by Gisela's fire-red mane as I was. She still hasn't forgiven Jordi for being the one who finally got Gisela's juices flowing.

A pointless grudge, in my humble opinion. After all, the one who chose between the two lovers (not counting me, of course; everyone on the *Gaudí* knows I don't go for females—not human females, anyway) was Gisela herself, right?

The worst of it is, apart from Amaya and Gisela and his own bad temper, Third Officer Barceló has his own reasons for feeling angry with me.

It's taken for granted that, given the peculiar nature of our trade, we condomnauts have certain . . . intimacy skills that can make a favorable impression on regular humans, to the point that some grow slightly addicted to our humble selves.

That may or may not be true, depending on the condomnaut. But the trouble is, all astronauts, who tend to be a pretty superstitious lot, believe it blindly. So it's taken for granted that if a Contact Specialist shows an obvious preference for any of the members of his crew, that favoritism will automatically generate awkward jealousies and suspicions in any small group of humans isolated for long periods. And a hyperjump ship crew is necessarily a small group of people.

So we've been ordered—well, to be fair, that's too strict a term, even for a directive from overbearing Miquel; let's say—it has been *earnestly recommended of us* that we try to "avoid certain group dynamics."

But what with the immensity of space, and how far we are from home, and how lonely watch duty can be, and how weak the flesh is, and on the other hand how hard and appetizing Jordi Barceló's flesh is . . .

The fact of the matter is, one night something on the not recommended list did happen. And it was definitely worth it.

With all that brawn, Jordi Barceló turned out to be quite the sex bomb. For a Catalan.

I enjoyed our hookup so much that I opened up to him that night, telling him a few things about my past that I tend not to let on to, such as the bit about Elpidio Valdés, one of my child-hood idols.

The catch was, the selfish brute then got the idea that he could enjoy my "services" every now and then—which wouldn't have been very disagreeable, after all—but also that I had to be his secret and exclusive property. Always be available, that is, for his and only his sexual whims. And without letting anyone else know about our arrangement, too.

Of course I refused that sort of secret slavery, but then the great big whiner went to the captain himself and accused me of having seduced and raped him—and him always such a strict heterosexual until I used my Caribbean wiles to lure him into the bunk, blah blah.

Ha. Needless to say, regardless of his feudal Catalan name, Captain Ramón Berenguer proved to be eminently just and open-minded. Instead of automatically siding with his fellow Catalan against the foreigner, he merely reminded Jordi in a voice dripping with irony and diplomatic tact that he, Jordi, stands six foot three and looks like Hercules' twin brother, whereas I'm barely five foot seven. So, Berenguer figured, the claim about a rape was just a crude lie from a spiteful lover.

As for getting himself seduced, good for him! Welcome to the flexible-views club. About time he gave up his narrow, old-fashioned ideas, which are especially anachronistic in an astronaut. The captain heartily congratulated him, because the life of a poor heterosexual on a ship crewed by women and men who are as bisexual as most humans in the twenty-second century must have been hell. Especially considering that three of the four women on the ship could hardly look at him without feeling an automatic urge to smack him.

The reprimand worked, of course. When a jealous, spiteful coworker tries to undermine you, it tends to help if you've had an earlier fling (brief but warm) with your captain.

I feel nervous as fuck. Still thinking about stuff that has nothing to do with Contact. As if the crew of this mountain-sized silver sphere cared about the gossip among our crew.

And what if they're telepaths? Shit.

Great first impression I'd be making.

But it's not like I can change the course of my rambling thoughts. I'm only human, damn it. Could you keep from thinking the word "rhinoceros" for fifteen seconds if you were told your life depended on not thinking it?

If so, then by all means, come trade places with me. For the good of all humanity, and especially of one very scared-shitless guy.

No takers? Just as I expected.

All up to me.

"Yes, I'm moving, Jordi. The *Dralgol* is a two-seater, and they must already have an estimate on our body size, so I just wanted to give them time to see that I'm here alone."

That's not good enough for the touchy bastard; in fact, the cure is worse than the disease. His close-shaven, big-jawed face trembles with offended dignity in the tiny holographic image inside my helmet visor.

"Don't call me Jordi, Cubanito! It's Third Officer Barceló to you. In fact, better make that Third Officer Barceló, *sir.*"

Yeah, my bad luck I went to bed with him. I won the elephant in the lottery, as Diosdado used to say.

Fortunately for me, Barceló's pompous scolding gets cut off by a swift series of flashing lights that come from the Alien ship, backed up by matching sounds. Smart idea: they don't know if we're a visual species. I can't make heads or tails of it, but the computer in my suit says it's a string of prime numbers (and presumably Jordi can confirm this on the Gaudí's computer if need be). The classical mathematical sequence, one that no natural process generates. Your typical Contact code.

Apparently they also think I'm dawdling.

As if to underscore the point, an entrance mysteriously opens at the bottom of the ship, down where it nearly touches ground. A huge entrance, like five hundred meters high. So this is how their vehicles were entering, those times when it looked like they were simply fusing with the ship: temporary hatches. Controlled surface tension, perhaps?

A sudden suspicion consequently strikes me: what if the entire ship isn't made of matter but energy, like my pet, Diosdadito?

Hell, why'd I have to think about my little pet? What I wouldn't give to be back home in Nu Barsa, safe and sound, playing with him.

But somebody's gotta put the frijoles on the table.

Hmm, energy. That could be why Amaya hasn't been able to pick out individual crew members on the ship: it's all energy, they're all energy. Living energy.

The possibility of understanding between creatures composed of matter—such as humans and almost all Aliens we've met so far—and creatures of pure energy are next to null. We simply move on different frequencies, even if we do so in the same universe.

Fortunately, so far we haven't discovered any intelligent energy-based species.

Or maybe Diosdadito is intelligent, and we just haven't figured it out yet.

For that matter, if he is, would he have noticed our reasoning ability?

Fragile bags of protoplasm—not like we'd seem rational to him.

Anyway. Then there's the even worse possibility of running into creatures made of antimatter.

That would make for a truly explosive Contact.

Good thing humanity hasn't gotten mixed up in such an incident, yet.

The Furasgans say they once went through that experience. It's not something they want to repeat.

Luckily, Amaya hasn't detected the peculiar sort of photon emissions you'd get from matter–antimatter annihilation, or any Cherenkov radiation. No, I shouldn't be thinking about antimatter, or energy, or even Diosdadito. Though . . . oh, how clearly I can picture him, moving with his beautiful, constantly shifting forms and colors along the ceiling of my comfy Nu Barsa apartment. At home. Every time I see that purring, affectionate, lazybones kitty Antares, it reminds me so much of him . . .

No, I shouldn't be thinking about my energy pet, or remembering Antares or Antares's owner. I should be concentrating on Contact. Empty your mind . . .

Okay, this is good: the sensors in my suit aren't picking up any changes in the electromagnetic fields of this XXXXXL-size ship. One less thing to worry about. Simple, solid, conventional matter. If these guys aren't pure energy, could it be a bioship, like the ones the Kigrans and the Algolese use? That also would render the biometer pretty much useless.

A chill runs down my back. Could be out of the frying pan, into the fire.

Last year I got to make Contact with the monstrous rorquals of Kigrai. That is, of Alpha Ophiuchi, according to the naming system of ancient Earth star charts. They also use biotech. But each individual grows up to half a kilometer long (females, slightly less). As if that's not enough, their genitalia are to scale.

That was a tough job, making that Contact. Ever since that day, I've had a rough idea of how a sperm feels inside a vagina.

Well, a Contact Specialist's job comes with thorns as well as roses.

That's why the few of us crazy enough to do it get paid the big bucks.

I keep moving with the mechanical industriousness of a beetle, climbing up a small ramp that has emerged from the opening. A welcome sign of courtesy. Apparently they realized that if I'm walking, I must not be able to fly.

The interior of the colossal Alien ship begins to glow a dull red. Lovely. Add some teeth and it'll remind me uncomfortably of a giant, hungry mouth. Or of another less often seen bodily opening with teeth, which I've always assumed was just a black legend in our profession.

Ah. Now it's not just glowing, it's pulsating. All it needs next is a voice howling, "Get inside already, idiot!"

Strangely, this starts to make me feel better about them. Big or small, at least they share one trait with us humans: impatience.

So, with my hands still in the air (hoping they don't interpret this as a threatening gesture), I sign off with Jordi and enter the bowels of the Alien ship. I even take the trouble to smile at his little holoimage. "I suppose we'll lose our connection when I go inside this Alien monster. Just in case: it was a pleasure working with you, Third Officer Barceló, *sir*. Say goodbye to Antares for me—and to Gisela."

His tiny face hardly moves a muscle when he replies, "Condomnaut Josué Valdés, I'll pass on your regards to my cat and my girlfriend. I hope to see you again, though. Really, I do. I'd hate it if anybody else took care of you. But just in case—*adieu*."

Yeah, that's real friendship for you.

Just as I guessed, it's a bioship. As soon as I'm inside, the ramp tucks itself away behind me and the entrance closes with remarkable fluidity. It seems like the opening never existed. At the same instant, the holographic window with Jordi's image goes haywire and flits off, and I'm left in a reddish, unmistakably organic penumbra.

My helmet sensors tell me the ammonia atmosphere of the planet outside is rapidly being replaced in here by oxygenated air. Could they have identified the kind of gas I breathe from the carbon dioxide I'm exhaling? These guys are good.

I start sweating and trembling again.

A test of professional self-discipline: don't think about the vagina dentata, don't think about . . .

Situation analysis: roughly spherical chamber, approximately two thousand meters in diameter; quite large, yet relatively insignificant in relation to the ship's total volume. If it's an airlock, or some sort of decontamination chamber, what does it lead to?

I can't see any other doors, though of course the interior layout of a bioship is incomparably elastic and flexible.

But you'd at least hope . . .

Dull red remains the predominant visible hue. Flesh, or what? Do they see better in infrared light? That would make sense: this nondescript little planet isn't exactly well-lit by the weak red star it has for a sun. There must be a reason they chose to stop here.

Well, hopefully I'll get a chance pretty soon to figure out why they did that, and many other things, too.

I recalibrate my helmet visors. Just in time.

A shadow is approaching. It's on the other side of the translucent membrane surrounding the chamber I'm in. A good guess is that the guys from the Contact's home team are stepping up to the plate.

Or the guy. Looks like there's just one of them. Well, in any case, here he is, passing through the last barrier. As he approaches, I take mental notes of his appearance with the swift precision gained from long practice.

What I can see at first blush bodes well: not too big; in fact, just about my height, which is always agreeably convenient. Bipedal posture. Two arms, two legs: definitely anthropoid. *¡Viva Shangó! ¡Viva Obbatalá!* One head, narrow waist, wide hips, large breasts—so this is a female. I generally prefer them when dealing with other species, maybe to make up for my forced abstention from human women for so many years. Though some Alien males or hermaphrodites aren't bad at all. Thin arms, long legs, blond hair . . .

Hair? And blond, to boot? Wow. Fortune isn't just smiling on me, it's grinning wide and laughing out loud.

No doubt about it: this Alien isn't just a female, she's 100 percent humanoid. And what a humanoid!

A perfect beauty, and not an inch of fabric covering her gloriously naked flesh.

Not just any woman, she's a Real Woman. Elegant, beautiful, voluptuous, refined, all in a single package. Extragalactic or not, this Contact Specialist could win any Miss Humanoid contest.

And to top it off, she reminds me of someone. How odd.

Yes. Someone I know very well. A model, an actress, a Nu Barsa holovision host? Now that I look at her, she reminds me a little of Nerys . . .

No. Definitely not. She doesn't even have green skin or gills. This isn't my mermaid, or any other Catalan public figure; she reminds me of someone from my more distant past, but also someone who was closer to me. Someone from my childhood, yes. From CH.

At last, I've got it. Of course: Evita!

Uh-oh. Turns out they're telepaths. How embarrassing. I hope they can take a joke. Or at least not consider it a capital crime. Evita . . . the little beauty, the only blond and blue-eyed girl in Rubble City, the daughter of Pablo Vargas, the greatly envied, powerful, arrogant director of Transplutonic Travels. A designer conception, she had been incubated in a sophisticated genetic womb up in Northia for a price that could have kept a hundred CH families living in luxury for practically a year. The rebellious hothouse flower who escaped her golden prison whenever she got the chance and played with us, the humble and happy orphans in the outer district.

And we watched over her, not just like she was our adopted little sister, but like she was made of glass. And not merely because we sensed that her father (what we wouldn't have given to have a father ourselves!), who prudently turned a blind eye to her adventures beyond the cage, would have boiled us alive if she came home with so much as a scratch on her perfect skin. Most of all, because it was such a pleasure to serve her, like knights serving their lady: helping her wade across the muddy stream, helping her hunt and maybe kill the enormous, omnipresent mutant scorpions, centipedes, and cockroaches that made her scream with fright and disgust, saving the best fruit that we stole from old blind Margot's garden for her.

Because even though we were just kids, she was even more of a child: she still had an innocence about her, while most of us already knew all about sex. And we were secretly thinking that when she grew up, having her as a girlfriend would be like being friends with the princess of heaven. So we were already trying to buy shares in the banking system of her affections. . . .

Or maybe it was just friendship. Clean, simple childhood friendship. Why not? If anything so pure and innocent could exist among the children of Rubble City, I mean.

Evita, my secret childhood crush. I suppose that, apart from my "little problem" with women, it was the memory of her and a slight resemblance between her face and Nerys's that made me fall for my snooty mermaid.

Evita, my forever impossible love. Right after I turned ten, some enterprising kids from the local chapter of the Pancaribbean Mafia kidnapped her, and her father decided not to pay the astronomical ransom they were demanding but instead to leave the neighborhood, abandoning her.

The next week she turned up dead in a rubbish dump. They had raped her first, of course. She was eight. The sort of thing that happens every day in CH—but all the same, what a pity. We all cried and cried over her, and maybe I cried more than most.

The upshot is, if Evita Vargas had survived to become a full-grown woman, she would have looked a lot like this extragalactic goddess.

Two and two make four. The creatures who control this ship, whether from the Milky Way or beyond, must be telepaths. A good thing, too. No matter how sophisticated the translation software behind my earplugs is (one of the few points of pride for our none-too-advanced human technology), it only works with known languages.

Oh, for the miraculous automatic translators that ancient science fiction writers used to depict. One of those would come in so handy for us condomnauts!

Apparently, just as they knew I breathe oxygen, these Aliens were able to extract the image of my childhood friend from my mind. And the speed with which they molded this adult version of her indicates that they're either natural shape-shifters or incredible biotech experts. As if the door and the entire ship don't already prove as much.

The situation isn't entirely unheard of: five years ago, the *Pravda Pobeda*, a neo-Russian scouting ship from the planet Rodina, made Contact with the Guzoids, colonizing polyps from a dark planet in a globular cluster in Radian 56, Quadrant 12. Near the equatorial constellation Sextans, I think. I don't quite recall whether Guzoids used spherical ships (in any case, the ship the Russians encountered must not have been as huge as this one, or they'd have made a note of it in their report). I do remember, though, that the uterus of the only sexed individual in the nest, the "queen," proved to be the most sophisticated genetic splicer yet discovered: it rapidly created several specialized individuals for making Contact that were such perfect imitations of humans that no one could have told them apart from us at first glance. And it did so just by looking, before gaining access to our precious DNA, a doubly impressive feat.

I figure the Russian condomnaut must have gone to town on that Contact, if he was lucky enough to get a partner even half as divine as this Alien pseudo-Evita standing now before me.

"No, Josué Valdés, we aren't extragalactic, nor are we the Guzoid polyps from Sextans you're thinking of. We haven't met them yet. But we have made Contact with a Qhigarian worldship that visited our home planet. They were the ones who sold us the Taraplin hyperengine that allowed us to reach this planet, along with a few facts about their species and others that are actively exploring the galaxy at this moment. That is the reason we did not come completely unequipped to this Contact." The contralto voice reaching me through the headphones in my suit is the sort of voice an angel must have, if angels exist: musical, melodious, at once innocent and sensual, with an accent that reminds me of the best of my childhood in CH.

And it's undoubtedly the voice Evita would have had, if she had grown up. At least, so far as I can remember. Maybe they're only partial telepaths, telereceivers, since so far they haven't sent me their thoughts, preferring to speak to me.

"No, we are in fact complete telepaths. And we are not bothered by jokes about us: obviously, we already have heard them all. In fact, we find the concept rather interesting. But we will discuss that, and many other things, we hope, later.

"But now we fear you will not be able to understand our thoughts. You can take off your helmet, however, Josué Valdés. Don't be afraid; as you have guessed, we picked up on your respiratory needs and have therefore modified the atmosphere around you. The air does not have any type of bacteria, virus, prion, or other pathogen that might harm your bodily functions, not even if your immune system were compromised."

Wow, really good telepaths. They're learning too much about us.

Every condomnaut facing a First Contact does so with a few little extra layers of protection. First, an immune system amped to the max. We stimulate our natural ability to repel infectious agents to such a degree, using biopharmaceuticals, that no bacteria can even survive in our intestines unless it shares at least 10 percent of our DNA.

It's a little uncomfortable, to be sure. Especially at first, with the constant diarrhea. But after a while you get used to it, and it's pretty reassuring to know you can reject almost any Alien parasite or pathogen that might make its way into your body without resorting to other drugs.

The second layer of protection is a little device we call the Countdown. The way it works is more or less incomprehensible for a layman like me, though for a change our human physicists have a better understanding of it than they do of hyperjump travel. This ingenious Algolese invention protects our valuable genetic heritage from being copied or stolen. When activated, it emits imperceptible ultrasonic vibrations that synchronize within an hour with the bearer's biofield, in such a way that the DNA of any cell that strays out of range will degrade in a matter of seconds.

This means that the vast majority of Contact Specialists use the device (some species can't withstand ultrasound waves and have to use other systems, which I don't know enough about to describe) so that they won't stay up at night worrying that the Aliens they make Contact with will get their hands on their most valuable treasure, the most treasured aspect of any species: their genetic code. Because if Aliens get your DNA, they can manipulate it (at least in theory) in the sort of unethical ways the Qhigarians are said to have used long ago to create entire slave-clone races.

Worn as a collar, the ultrasound transmitter has become the hallmark of my profession. In fact, one of the many theories circulating about the origins of the humorous nickname everybody calls us by is that it comes from the pronunciation of the English word Countdown as we hispanicized it: countdown, coundóun, *condón*, "condom."

Contact Specialists: condom-nauts.

Personally, I find this hypothesis is as good as any other. As an Italian might say, *se non è vero, è ben trovato*. More or less: "maybe it's not true, but it makes a good story."

Anyway, they call us *condomnautas*. Maybe it sounds better in Spanish. But the truth is, it's all talk: things have changed a little since the day Quim Molá pulled on a real condom, and nowadays we usually make Contact without any physical protection other than our own skin. No rubbers. What sense does it make? After all, nobody worries about getting pregnant from "sleeping" with an Alien.

"Thanks," I say to my statuesque counterpart, keeping it short (words aren't really necessary when you're dealing with a complete telepath). I open the valve on my helmet before taking it off and for the first time breathe in the Alien air—which indeed proves to be completely odorless. They understand our respiratory parameters as well as we do ourselves.

I'm starting to get over my disappointment about missing the huge bonus I would have made for making First Contact with extragalactic Aliens. I lost the bonus, but today is still my lucky day. A humanoid! Miss Human Sphere! What a babe! And she looks like Evita, too—a childhood erotic fantasy made real. I'm one lucky guy. Who cares if she's not a real human, when I've got such a fantastic Contact waiting for me?

Well, *I* care, of course. If she really were human, I wouldn't be able to function, either as a Contact Specialist or as a man. That's the cross I bear, and at the same time it's the best thing I have going for me and the source of my greatest talent.

Naturally, nobody on the *Gaudí* knows this, and nobody in Nu Barsa either except for jolly old Narcís Puigcorbé. But I can count on his discretion, whether or not he finally retires this year.

I also toss the translation earplugs and am more than ready to kick off the rest of my suit as soon as I can. One good thing about even the most heavily armored condomnaut suits is how easy they are to remove. A necessity for doing the job right, of course.

However, when a beauty like this, no matter how Alien she might be (or rather, precisely because she's so Alien), steps up to help me remove this little obstacle between her flesh and mine, everything becomes much simpler—and much more enjoyable.

"We hail from the third star in the constellation that you call Crater, the Cup. It is a quintuple blue sun with no planets. Radian 3278, Quadrant 6 in the current cartography. We are a unitary being, made not of energy but of an elastic bioplasm that evolved in the system's thin asteroid ring," the lovely pseudo-Evita tells me, while gently fingering the Countdown collar with her perfect hand as soon as I am as naked as she.

No wonder the biometer couldn't distinguish one crew member from another inside the ship: the whole ship is a single entity. Not a bioship but a creature capable of traveling among the stars. Making Contact with Aliens is a source of constant surprises, and it forces you to rethink what had seemed to be the most solid paradigms.

Another reason I love this job.

The gorgeous unitary being continues her speech, warm but fearless. "We assimilate radiant energy directly, and given our form of metabolism, we are virtually immortal, so we reproduce only rarely, by budding or fission. Therefore, the diplomatic ritual of Contact through sexual intercourse, of Taraplin origin, which almost every life form in this galaxy observes, strikes us as fairly . . . meaningless." If she's extracting all these words from my mind, she's doing a good enough job of arranging them to sound convincingly human. That body and that face help a bit, too, of course. "Nevertheless, we are prepared to respect the tradition, just as we respected it on our First Contact with the Qhigarians. This . . . humanoid body, which we have molded based upon your memories, is only a partial projection, intended to facilitate your physical interaction with us. Shall we proceed, Josué Valdés?" Her final words follow the proper Protocol for First Contact. Maybe she learned them from the Qhigarians, maybe she grabbed from my brain; who cares.

I'm all for keeping the old traditions, this once. In fact, right now I'm a stickler.

I approach the fascinating "partial projection" of the Alien single bioplasm unit and tell her, in my most loving voice, something that could not have been very clear in my thoughts: "She was Evita to me, but perhaps as a species you would prefer to be known by some more formal name."

"Excellent." Her words ring in my mind, not my ears. "We shall be the Evita Entity."

Well, there's more than one way to leave your mark on history. I won't be the first or the last Contact Specialist to do so, whether by chance or by design. Since the Five Minute War, almost all of human history for the past half century bears the stamp of the condomnauts.

Josué Valdés, Contacter of the Evita Entity. I rather like the sound of it.

Reciprocating her earlier gesture, now I am the one placing my hand on her delicate neck. It's pure heaven, her rosy skin trembling under my fingertips. It's just as silky soft as I remember it. I spend nearly ten seconds simply enjoying the feeling, then at last I say the ritual words, my libido quaking with every syllable: "Welcome therefore to the realm of humanity and of the Nu Barsa enclave, Evita Entity. May this First Contact and its intercourse mark the beginning of a fruitful trading relationship between our species. Let us proceed."

And, wow, do we ever proceed. My hand slips down to her erect breasts, I kiss her, embrace her, and slowly we let ourselves fall to the floor in a tight knot of arms and legs. I have a huge erection. Thinking of how human she looks without being human in reality is the best aphrodisiac I could imagine.

So everything goes wonderfully well. Even before her thighs hit the soft organic floor, I'm inside her, and for a long time, as we move in unison, rolling across the bioplasmic bed, I feel her, wet, soft, exquisitely welcoming . . .

I'm nine years old, skinny, grubby, barefoot, half naked, surrounded by other kids as filthy as me. We're in a muddy, unpaved little street that's baking in the sun, flanked by shanties cobbled together from plastic paneling and recycled sheets of galvanized iron.

The street is named Tu Madre También. "So's Your Mother" Street. It's the main thoroughfare of Rubble City, the most impoverished district on the outskirts of CH, the beggar-queen metropolis, capital of poverty-stricken post-Five-Minute-War Cuba. The place I swear I'll never come back to so long as I live. And to which I return regardless, night after night, in my recurrent nightmares.

So I know this is a dream. For all the good it does me. All the good it ever does me. I can't wake up. Much less control what's happening to me. The worst thing is, since this isn't the first time I've relived this scene, I already know everything that comes next.

It's a tragicomedy, being stuck in your own body, in your own past, which keeps repeating over and over until . . . until when?

As always, unaware of any drama, I jump around, make a racket, scream and shout along with all the other kids, like any poor but happy kid anywhere in the world would do, with the excitement you only feel when the games are about to begin.

Because we're going to play—and I know full well what it is we'll be playing.

Several of us are holding small multicolored cages woven from braided polystyrene fibers. These aren't industrial products but a sampling of homemade children's handicrafts that we've skillfully fashioned out of rubbish patiently recovered from the huge trash mounds surrounding Rubble City. Some kids even manage to sell them to outsiders, six for a CUC—the devalued Cuban monetary unit dating back, I'm told, to the early twenty-first century.

And inside those handwoven cages, we've got our runners.

I haven't looked at them yet. I'd rather concentrate on the characters from my early years, who in this dream look exactly like I remember them.

It's like settling a debt I owe to my nostalgia for a childhood I'll never get back. Fortunately.

Here's Yamil Check-My-Biceps, the bronze-skinned, green-eyed kid with the kinky hair who, at the tender age of twelve, is bursting with pride in his steroidal muscles. Well-dressed, attractive in the dangerous way bad kids can be. Kids born wicked. Not that I ever found him attractive, sexually speaking.

He always beat up on the little kids and dreamed of the big ones letting him into their gang. He'll die without ever getting there, at the age of fifteen, from an overdose of wildwall. For now, though, he's alive and kicking right here in front of me, showing off his magnificent Afro.

Standing next to him is his shadow, his scale-model replica, down to the miniature Afro, looking up at him like a minion at his god: his little brother, Yotuel Fullmouth. He hardly ever speaks and always keeps himself meticulously clean and good-smelling. He likes to dress in pristine white clothes, though he's not a yabó. People say he pays for his beloved older brother's vices and pleasures with the CUCs he picks up at night, sucking off the lonely, rich old men who park in the highway rest stop near Rubble City. Apparently, if you want to attract those perverted fat cats, you've got to smell really good and look healthy.

Yeah, life is hard here in CH, and everybody deals with it as best they can, without judging anybody else.

Evita is here, too, of course. Not up front but in back of the crowd. She's just six now, and her blond hair and blue eyes contrast almost comically with the thick layer of dirt clinging to her milk-white skin. Amazing how much grime she's managed to get on her in just two hours since she escaped her house.

Later, so she can get back into her good clothes without making her strict father, Big Boss Vargas, suspicious about her running away, Abel and I will have to bathe her conscientiously, happily wasting the water that we worked so hard that morning to haul up, bucket by bucket, from the only unpolluted potable water tap in the neighborhood, energetically scrubbing her while she laughs with delight and not a trace of shame, never suspecting that we're no longer staring at her naked body quite as innocently as we had the year before.

Abel, my best friend. Mi amigo del alma. The first kid I secretly shared the pleasures of sex with, our mutual discovery of having an orgasm, which was more than an extension of our friendship. Skin as black as night, soul as pure as heaven. I wouldn't be where I am today if not for him. At the age of fifteen, as soon as his born skill with computers began to pay its first dividends, he loaned me the money for my ticket into orbit, trusting that someday I'd pay him back.

I have no idea what's become of him. When I climbed on board the shuttle to the Clifford Simak Geosynchronic Transit Station, those *thousand CUCs seemed like a fortune, and I promised to give them back to him as soon as I could. But eight years have gone by, I've made a thousand times that much money, and I've never even tried.*

I'm an ungrateful, egotistical bastard, I know.

Maybe he's already dead, Abel. The life of a hacker in Rubble City isn't worth much. The Pancaribbean Mafia considers them disposable personnel.

Or maybe he left his risky job, got married, has kids of his own, and . . .

But no, I can't let myself think about such things, not even in my dreams.

Also jumping around and making a racket with the rest of us is Little Ramiro Flyface, the boy who was born without eyes because his mother abused broncodust when she was pregnant with him. The funny thing is that after he was born, Lina became the best mother in the world (maybe she felt guilty), and for years she saved up every CUC she earned from selling her body until, when her son was five, she was able to buy him the artificial eyes he needed. They might have been the cheapest on the market, a pair of multifaceted North Korean holoprostheses that only let him see in black and white and gave him his nickname, but all the same he preferred it to what they used to call him: Little Ramiro Flatface.

And here's Yamy, a glowingly healthy, precocious girl, the only professional worker in the neighborhood. Professional sex worker, that is. She's with Marré el Gordo's housecall girls. At the age of eight, she's already forgotten more about sex than most women in Nu Barsa will learn in their whole lives. The nipples of her skinny breasts, still more those of a child than of an adolescent, barely covered by a thin T-shirt, translucent as onionskin, are more expressive than her big, mascara-coated eyes. She glances at me every now and then, mischievously. She's promised me that when I turn ten in a few months, she'll initiate me for free into the mysteries of hetero sex, and I won't have to go through the sweaty, greasy ordeal so many other boys endure with lusty Karlita.

She'll never fulfill that promise. The brilliance of nocturnal butterflies fades quickly in Rubble City, and Marré el Gordo pays well—but only because he doesn't do much to keep his girls safe. Some dissatisfied client will let something slip about Yamy's perfect health, a very valuable exception in the polluted environment of CH; organ traffickers from the Pancaribbean Mafia will catch her one night on her way home from making the rounds, and all we'll find later will be the remains.

The police? Don't bother. The easiest way to keep law and order in CH is to pretend the outer districts simply don't exist and let us kill each other ourselves.

There's also Ricardito, nicknamed the Octopus because some nasty trick of chemistry, radioactivity, and sensitive genes made him be born with two tiny extra hands jutting from his elbows. No surgeon dares to amputate them, for fear that doing so might make him lose mobility in his regular hands.

Also, there's the one I'll never forget. Slow and easygoing because of the extra weight her mutant metabolism gives her, sweating acrid buckets from every pore, there's Karlita the Tub, who later on will always remind me of my friend Narcís—though he's well over seven feet tall and he lets himself weigh three hundred kilos from pure laziness, while Karlita, like it or not, already weighs two hundred kilos at the age of eight, and she's barely five foot four.

Worse, the poor girl knows her condition will worsen year by year until she finally suffocates under her own rolls of fat before turning twenty-five. So, wishing to make the most of her short life span, she's always available for the craziest sex games.

And there's Damián, better known as Legs the Orphan. So-called because his father, hooked on wildwall, the curse of our neighborhood (one of many; here, drugs grow like weeds), sold his son's legs to an organ trafficker when the kid was three. After the father came down from his high, he felt so ashamed he killed himself. He left behind Rita, a pay guide dog he'd picked up cheap when Aid for the Disabled discarded it for being a mutant. Not so much for its three eyes as for always being in heat.

In other words, the whole gang's here. Because today is Racing Day.

Not horse racing, of course. Not dog racing, or steroid-pumped human racing like you can see on holovision or in the fancy stadiums of luxurious downtown CH. No. Here in Rubble City, the populated zone with the highest background radioactivity level anywhere on our already polluted planet Earth, none of those well-trained or genetically engineered runners would last one day.

The tenement house where I grew up is a hellhole at the end of the tunnel. Only the most desperate or the most highly resistant creatures can survive there. No wonder, then, that both the poor little mutants that do the racing and we humans who do the betting on them are all amply endowed with resistance and with desperation.

Boasting, howling, and pounding on one another's backs, half-jokingly and half deadly serious, like mischievous or perhaps lecherous monkeys, those of us who've brought our little cages end up in the front row, ready to set our captives loose when old Diosdado gives the signal.

Diosdado Valdés, heart and soul of So's Your Mother Street and respected throughout Rubble City, is the adoptive father or grand-father—nobody knows which and nobody cares—of dozens of orphans. He takes in lots of newborns abandoned by their mothers, raising them and watching over them in his home to repay his orishas for the generosity someone showed him when he was little. Until they're five and can fend for themselves. Then he frees us, to die in the streets—or grow into adults.

But all of us who survived were proud to bear his last name, which he told us was, once upon a time, the only surname fatherless children were allowed to bear in Cuba.

The old man is one of the most highly respected babalawos, priests in the syncretic Yoruba religion of the orishas, in all Rubble City. Some say, in all CH. Nobody knows how old he really is. They say that though he now seems like a harmless fellow, he was in Special Ops when he was young, and he got injured in an explosion. They also say he sacrificed part of his body to the jealous African deities. It might all be true. He's thin, always wears white, has only one eye and one leg, and constantly jokes that any day now he'll cut off an arm to finally look like his favorite orisha: one-legged, one-eyed, one-armed Olofi. Diosdado is the only adult whose authority we kids unquestioningly recognize is the eternal judge and arbiter of our most serious games and arguments.

"*Goddamn kids, stop screwing around and set your racers on the tracks! Helpers, put out the sugar!*" *Diosdado thunders in his rum-soaked bass, an incongruously deep tone for someone as short and thin as him, while he hobbles over on his bullwood crutch.*

"*Josué, guess what: Diosdado has a 'hey, man' body and a 'yes, sir' voice!*" *Evita whispers mischievously into my ear, clever as always. She plants a wet kiss on my cheek before adding,* "*I want Atevi to win. I know you named her after me.*"

Evita, Atevi. Obvious, isn't it? Even a six-year-old girl could figure it out.

I don't answer her, just place the cage holding my hopes of victory on the starting line. Across the way, at other end of the galvanized steel tracks, my buddy Abel, who is serving as my helper today, is spreading the sugar to attract my racer and her rival.

"*For the first race: place your bets!*" *Diosdado bellows, and the roar of the crowd redoubles.*

Yotuel Fullmouth, moving with a dancer's grace not to dirty his unsullied white clothes, silently takes his place next to Abel. All the other kids point and laugh when he pulls on a pair of long rubber gloves, just in case.

Yamil's younger brother has never been able to take these races. It's almost a phobia with him. He still screams sometimes when one of the creatures gets too close to him. Acting as his brother's helper in this race is the best proof he could give of his love for him. He's obsessed with cleanliness: he's the only person in the neighborhood who bathes two or three times a day and throws off his clothes as soon as they start to stink.

I understand now that he didn't do it just to appear attractive to his "clients." It was because his work made him feel dirty all the time.

The champ to beat in Rubble City for the past few months, and therefore the first to compete, is Centella, Yamil's racer. Some say he shares his steroids with her, and maybe it's true: she's not as big as my Atevi, but her legs are long and she runs like she's got fire in her belly.

"Six CUCs on my Centella!" howls Yamil Check-My-Biceps, proudly tossing his Afro and waving a muscle-bound fist full of old debit cards and subcutaneous chips, stolen or found in the trash, as if they held millions of CUCs and not a few miserable pennies. Six CUCs is a respectable amount in Rubble City, though. People have been killed for less. A lot less. Who will accept his challenge?

As if he didn't know. As if he didn't see Abel standing next to Yamil's brother. As if I didn't exist.

Murmuring. Everybody looks at me; they know what I promised, I can't take it back now, but . . .

"Go ahead, Josué. If you lose, I'll loan you the money. My papá *leaves more than that on his chips when he changes them at the end of every month," Evita whispers. And from the finish line, Abel smiles and winks at me: Atevi is as ready as she'll ever be. It's now or never.*

I swallow hard and say simply, "You're on."

"This little kid? Josué?" Yamil smirks, cocky, as if he hadn't seen me until now and hadn't known for weeks about my plan to challenge his supremacy. "A little bleached-out mulatto like you? Such

a nobody that even your friends call you Zero? You're planning to beat my champ with that albino monster of yours?" He laughs, and half the neighborhood laughs with him, starting with his quiet little brother. *"Drop it, bro. I don't have waste to time on your bullshit. Take your white bug and come back here and bet with the men when you and your bug have grown up a little—and gotten some color, too. Zero."*

Ruthless laughter. Again I swallow hard; it's true that they call me Zero, but that's because I got lice when I was five and Diosdado decided to deal with it by shaving me bald, "to cure me healthy."

Like so many other kids in the neighborhood, you know. Except with me, the nickname stuck.

"If I lose, I'll pay up," I say in a thin voice, cursing the day I lost the genetic lottery by not being born with a bass baritone like Diosdado's—or skin as tan as the two brothers with their Afros, not to mention almost everyone else in the neighborhood. "With real money."

"Real money?" Yamil Check-My-Biceps continues showing off. His green eyes glint almost maliciously under his implausibly scraggly blond Afro. "I don't doubt it, Zero. If I had a blue-eyed goose that lays the golden egg like the bird standing by your side, a daddy's little girl, I'd also have me some real money. But what if I don't want your CUCs after I beat your albino? What if I want the goose herself?"

I drape my arm protectively across Evita's shoulders. No. No way. She isn't part of the deal. I don't even want to think about what Yamil might do to her. Fuck, things are spinning out of control.

According to the pitiless rules of the neighborhood, the champion can decide on the bet, and the challenger can refuse to accept it—up to three times. If he refuses a fourth offer, he's considered to have lost the challenge without contest.

"Yamil, that's enough," my black brother Abel quietly says from the other side of the tracks, his voice low but firm, so everyone can hear him. "Six CUCs aren't worth one of Evita's snot balls. Ask for something else."

"Something else? Okay, let's see." He pretends to think it over, ostentatiously running his fingers through his bushy, blond, exuberant Afro. "Let's see. How about, if his bleached bug loses, little Josué Zero will have to fuck whoever I choose?"

"Sounds fair—so long as the other person wants it, too," Abel snarls, apparently more certain of our victory than I am, and everybody laughs.

My friend, always so good at manipulating people, has worked his miracle again with just a few words. Now the crowd doesn't want to watch Check-My-Biceps humiliate me again; they're on my side, rooting for the underdog, siding with David against Goliath. That's always the story of my island.

For all the good it'll do me. Even with everybody cheering him on, David wouldn't have brought down Goliath if he had left his sling at home. Is my cheering section going to help Atevi run faster? Or, if I lose (hope not! but it's a possibility, for sure), will their tears keep me safe from Yamil?

And what does Check-My-Biceps have in mind for me, anyway? I've been here before. I already know where this dream is heading, but I still can't believe he'd want me to . . .

Better not think about it, if you don't want it to happen, Diosdado always says.

"Sure," Yamil agrees, biting his lips in spite. It isn't what he had hoped for, but he knows the rules of the race give him no choice. "Otherwise it would be rape, and I don't think our little friend Zero could rape his own shadow. We gonna race, then?"

"Let's race," I say, sounding as sure of myself as I can, and I place my cage with Atevi on the starting line.

All Check-My-Biceps can do is imitate me, and there we stand, eager, staring at each other, eyes ablaze. But the bodybuilder's almost adult hatred is nothing compared to the pure uncut rancor silently throbbing in the green pupils of his little brother at the other end of the tracks.

Oh, there's no hate like childhood hate.

I wonder what happened to little Yotuel later on. For some reason, no one knows why, he will blame me when Yamil dies. Highway boy prostitute at the age of eight, no brawny big brother to protect him; his life must have gotten pretty hard. And then he disappeared from the neighborhood.

Never to return, I suspect. Maybe he died shortly thereafter, like so many other kids of my generation in Rubble City, orphans or not. I can't picture him as an adult, obsessed as he was with cleanliness but having to live surrounded by shit.

But my dream keeps moving ahead, giving me no time for my pessimistic reflections.

"On your mark! Set! Release your bugs, idiots!" Diosdado shouts in his bass baritone.

And off go the racers, to the frenzied shouts of the crowd.

The regulation racing tracks are gutters made of smooth galvanized steel, fifteen centimeters deep, walls highly polished so the racers can't climb out. They're eight meters long, with two curves and three hills and valleys bent into them.

They are easy to scrounge from the garbage dumps in Rubble City. Years later, I'll figure out that they're made from the scrapped exhaust pipes of old Chinese-manufactured rocket engines, cut in half lengthwise.

My Atevi is better trained than Yamil's Centella. While her rival, the reigning champion, wastes a couple of precious seconds exploring the starting gate and getting her bearings in time and space, my challenger has already smelled the sugar at the other end of the track and, waving her long antennae aloft, run almost half a meter, moving as fast as her six spiny, chitinous legs can carry her.

Abel winks at me. Yotuel and Yamil look like shit; I'm all smiles, listening to Evita laugh uproariously by my side, literally jumping up and down in excitement. Bravo, Atevi! I didn't go wrong when I picked you from all the others in your brood. You're a natural competitor.

Right. Though I clipped her wings like we always do before we start training racers, she even raises her milky-white elytra as if to release her flying apparatus. Oh, if only she could fly—then there'd be no doubt she'd get there first, long before Centella.

Maybe someday they'll figure out how to do flying races, and then they won't have to continue mutilating the finest mutant cockroaches in the neighborhood.

Years later, as a respected condomnaut in Nu Barsa, when I have the time and the means to learn about these and many other things, when I round out my feeble education by reading everything that falls into my hands, I'll find out that her scientific name is Periplaneta americana mutantis. *And that her species has lived among humans since time immemorial, being almost universally considered the most disgusting insect and one of the most repugnant creatures in the world, to the point that some psychologists believe our rejection of her kind is fixed in our genes at birth.*

But they're wrong. Or perhaps it's that human beings can adapt to practically anything. Back then—right now, in my dream—Yotuel is the exception to the rule; for me, and for almost all the Valdés orphans, they're not pests, they're just cockroaches, giant bugs, racers. We don't see them as repulsive monsters. Instead, we respect them as natural survivors that appeared along with lots of other mutant creatures after background radiation spiked with the Five Minute War.

Nor do they stink. If you raise them in a clean environment from the time they're tiny, they just have a faint spicy smell. Like my Atevi.

At just under five inches long, my racer would be a perfect specimen of her highly resistant species, if not for the fact that something twisted her genes and she lost her pigmentation. If you hold her up against the light, you can see through her chitin and watch her rapid heartbeat, the gastric juices moving in her intestine when she eats, her muscles flexing and extending.

A lovely show. Or a disgusting display, depending on whether it's Abel or me or finicky Yotuel observing her.

Of course, Atevi is far from the largest cockroach we've ever found in Rubble City. I myself have seen some that measure eight inches. Bugs that fight with dogs over bones in the street. Diosdado swears that once when he was young, he saw one half a meter long, meowing like a cat. But we all think that's just a tall tale, like the ones about the titanic meter-long insects that were supposedly exterminated in Rot Town.

Later on I'll find out we were right to be skeptical. Like all insects, cockroaches lack lungs. They breathe through their trachea, an efficient system—for small animals. An insect as big as Diosdado's would simply asphyxiate. Not to mention that exoskeletons, a lightweight and efficient support system for tiny creatures, also become inefficient and cumbersome when bugs grow beyond a certain size, until at last they cannot even support their own weight.

As kids in Rubble City, maybe we intuitively guessed something of the sort. We all knew that when racers are six inches or longer, they get so heavy they can barely fly or run.

The best racers are long-legged ones, like Centella, who's a little under five inches, but with her long shanks she looks like my Atevi's little sister on stilts.

Oh, damn those long legs. By meter two of the steel race track, she's making up for lost ground. The bitch is a natural runner. By meter four, she's left Atevi behind. Afro Boy gets his sarcastic, arrogant smile back. God, I hate him. Evita falls silent and stops jumping up and down, watching me in dismay, as if she can't believe what's happening.

But for an insect, even one five inches long, eight meters of race track with three hills to climb up and down is almost like a marathon for a human. Speed isn't the only decisive factor; in the end, it also takes endurance.

I've trained my Atevi by making her run up to fifteen meters without a rest, using gentle electric shocks. Though later, on the coldest nights,

I also let her snuggle up to me for warmth when she sleeps, while I enjoy the smell of her. Velvet glove on an iron fist.

Apparently, whether or not he shares his steroids with her, Yamil hasn't bothered to do anything of the kind with his racer. In the final meter, Centella flags again, her rhythm slows, and my translucent beauty closes the gap once more.

The roar of the crowd grows deafening. Pandemonium: everybody around me is jumping and screaming. Evita squeezes my hand, hard. All I can look at is my supercockroach, and less than half a meter from the finish line she catches up to the champion . . . passes her . . . No! Centella puts on a last spurt, her spindly legs squeal along the galvanized steel. Now it's antenna and antenna.

But Yamil's long-legged racer raises her elytra, lets out a pair of sloppily clipped wings (it seems that caring for animals, despite all the money he gets from them, isn't Afro Boy's strong suit), and though she can't quite manage flight, the extra push from her clumsy flapping gets her to the sugar prize first. Just by a couple of millimeters, but she has definitely won the race.

Yamil Check-My-Biceps falls to his knees, raises his brawny arms to the sky and howls in victory. His quiet brother runs over to hug him, enjoying his share of triumph (though all the while keeping a prudent distance from the repugnant Centella). Abel and I run to Diosdado to protest, gesticulating wildly. "It has wings, it has wings, invalidate the race, that's cheating!"

"I'm not invalidating a goddamn thing," the old babalawo pronounces stonily in his incontrovertible bass voice. "It didn't fly, so it's not disqualified. Josué, you have to pay up."

Abel sighs, looks at me, and nods. There's no way out. I sigh.

Afro Boy gives me that sarcastic look, then calls out, delighting in his authority, "Karlita, Tub, slut, sweet thing, come over here. I've got a surprise for you."

The obese mutant approaches with her potbellied waddle, sweaty and lubricious, licking her lips and reaching out to me with her eager hands, which look like bunches of overstuffed sausages.

"Shit, I'd ten times rather fuck Damián's old dog Rita than that fat lardbucket," Abel admits in his thin voice, whispering into my ear, perhaps to encourage me.

And this is where the real nightmare begins.

In real life, nobody but me could hear Abel's comment, so I had to put on a brave face, be a good loser, and act like a man: at the age of eight, try to get up a regular erection while faced with Karlita's kilos upon kilos of naked, quivering flesh and her pungent, acrid odor. And do it in front of everybody, pumping her to the sound of their cheers and jeers, thinking about Yamy and Evita for several interminably long minutes, until Check-My-Biceps declared himself satisfied with the pathetic spectacle.

Screw cockroaches, this is what repugnant really means. Of course I don't have an orgasm.

Worse: from that day on, I've never been able to get excited in the presence of a completely human woman.

Yes, completely human, because whatever other people might say, that's what Karlita was, all two hundred kilos of her. Fat girls have feelings, too, damn it. Not her fault she was born that way.

I mean, I'm not a total idiot. I don't blame her. I blame that fucking

Yamil. But knowing that Check-My-Biceps and his sick brain engineered it all doesn't help me get over my complexes.

In fact, as sorry as it sounds, if I found myself stranded on a classic desert island alone with the most beautiful woman in the universe and that asshole Yamil—much as I hate him, I'd rather go with him than with the goddess.

Worse, I'd rather screw the inevitable lonesome palm tree that all those desert isles have than a woman. And if my attack on her self-esteem drove her to suicide—tough luck.

Pity I've never made Contact with a vegetable species, isn't it? So far.

Strictly speaking, then, I should be grateful to that bastard Yamil for giving me a profession along with a dose of trauma. Though he restricted my choice of partners to males and, platonic relationships such as my obsession over the Gaudí's hypernavigator Gisela aside, to fairly non-human phenotypes, such as the second-generation condomnaut Nerys, with her mermaid fins and gills.

Anyhow, if Nerys asks me to go all the way with her someday, I'm afraid I'll vomit.

But in my recurrent nightly dream, things turn out different: green-eyed Afro Boy hears my friend's comment and offers me an unexpected alternative.

"That's okay, Zero, I'll let you have a try at it. Don't like the fatty? Well, there's Legs Damián's skinny dog Rita—take her! Right here, in front of everybody!"

So I suddenly find my raggedy shorts, the only clothing I ever wear, down around my ankles, while I'm holding on to a muscular back, the short rough hairs bristling with pleasure, and humping my hips against the Doberman's moist hindquarters.

The worst thing every night is that, with the typical illogic of nightmares, each time I move my hips the dog seems to grow and transform around my childish genitals, gradually turning into a strange hybrid of mutant dog and fat human female, of Rita and Karlita, who turns her head to look at me with her three sardonic eyes; her mouth half-open, she lets her tongue loll luxuriantly between her sharp canines and whispers to me, "Like that, Josué, give it to me hard, harder . . ."

And I can't wake up until, after a long struggle against the horrid nightmare, I emerge from the depths of sleep with a shriek, drenched in sweat.

What I hate is that every night I can stand it for a little bit longer.

Just now, for example, the horrifying dog-woman chimera is telling me, for the first time since I've had this recurring nightmare, "Cojons, Josué, get up and open for me, bastard! I didn't exactly come here to talk to you about colorful fish."

Talk to me about colorful fish? What?

And cojons? *I think that's Catalan.*

Stop right there. Karlita never would have said that. Tubs didn't speak Catalan.

That had to be . . . that is . . . Narcís. Yes. Narcís Puigcorbé. A sight for sore eyes.

I'm not eight, I'm twenty-three. This isn't Rubble City, it's Nu Barsa.

I got you, subconscious. Dream's over for today.

I emerge from my deep slumber with a long groan of relief. I wake up, as I always have for the past few years, on my stomach, my hands clenched as if grasping something. If I didn't sleep floating naked on an antigrav board, my fingers would now be tightening around my bedclothes as if to strangle them.

I had to buy this overpriced Algolese bed to keep from spending a fortune constantly replacing the mattresses, pillows, sheets, and covers I shredded night after night. And to keep from waking up drenched in my own sweat. Now the droplets float weightlessly around me. Nice.

But I think there's a lot fewer drops today than other nights. That's progress.

Enough to raise my hopes I may get over it in the near future.

Let's say, optimistically, at some point in the next two thousand years.

A few centimeters from my face, my Catalan condomnaut friend's enormous humanity is squeezed into a twenty-inch hologram. I watch him gesticulating impatiently at my door.

It's just nine in the morning. Disgusting.

The AI that controls my home has instructions to wake me at this ridiculous hour only if one of three people is calling or visiting: Nerys, my mermaid girlfriend; Miquel Llul, the feared head of the Nu Barsa Department of Contacts; and this fat fellow with the heart of gold, or his wife, Sonya.

"Coming, damn it, you elephantine early riser," I grumble. Then I yawn, lazily turning over to enjoy the effect of the gesture in weightlessness. "Whatever you're bringing better be really important."

"*Cojons*, Josué, don't be such a fucking narcissist. Wrap up your damn exercises. At this rate, you won't get to the Central del Govern till the day after tomorrow," Narcís says while stuffing his face, as he does whenever he has half a chance.

This time he's eating pork tamales. Not the slop that pops out of the autochef (a German invention, of course; when were there ever any good German chefs?), but real tamales that I made myself. In a real kitchen. Following the old Rubble City recipe.

"You people don't know anything about punctuality, but man, you sure know how to cook!" my friend says with his mouth full, polishing off the last tamale.

Ymala, who taught me how to make them, died when she was ten. Broncodust.

"Chill, Fats," I mutter, absorbed in finishing my last series of bench presses with the variable gravity bar, now set to a respectable 115 kilos. "Gimme time . . . After all . . . it's officially just . . . five minutes since . . . I got the . . . urgent call . . . Won't look good if . . . I get there first . . . now, will it?"

Allergic to anything that smells like physical exertion, the expansive Catalan condomnaut looks on with visceral disapproval as, bathed in sweat, I replace the ingenious device on its stand. "I don't know why you insist on this nonsense, Cubanito," he points out, again. "At your age, with your complexion and your undernourished past, and refusing to use steroids, you'll never have a hot bod or win Mr. Nu Barsa. So what's the point?"

"It helps me . . . to think," I only half-lie to him, as I lie on the bench doing pec flies with the variable gravity dumbbells, dialed down to a manageable twenty kilos.

In Rubble City, since I was the age when any boy with an imagination aspires to grow up to be a brawny he-man and look like a superhero (for example, like that nasty, unbearable, but delicious specimen of masculinity, Jordi Barceló), I dreamed of having a set of gym equipment like this.

My set of ultratech variable gravity bars handily replaces a roomful of traditional weights while taking up much less space. They're superlight when turned off, so I can take them with me almost anywhere. The only drawback, for a poor kid from Rubble City, is that like all sophisticated devices, especially those that use Alien technologies such as Algolese gravity control, they're almost a hundred times more expensive.

So one of the first things I did when I became a Contact Specialist in Nu Barsa eight years ago and got my first credit chip was to run out and make a childhood dream come true by buying this superadvanced gym set.

It isn't totally wrong to say exercise helps me to think. Mainly to think about how far I've come since I was a starving brat on the streets of Rubble City, CH. And about how much it cost me to get here and how far I'll go to keep this life. And acquire more stuff, if I can.

On the other hand, it's true that I'll never look like the third officer of the hyperjump frigate *Antoni Gaudí*, much less like the professional bodybuilders he used to work out with. Human mounds of genetic privilege, two hundred kilos of pure muscle and barely 5 percent body fat, sweating and panting in the enclave's gyms, metabolisms so altered by hormone and steroid cocktails that they rarely live to see the age of sixty.

I'll pass. But I'm not planning on becoming a flabby mass like my elephantine friend Puigcorbé, either. And if it sounds like I'm making a big deal of his weight, well . . . yeah. I am. Can't help it. That's how it is. Like, I love the guy, but I'm not blind: he's fat. Gargantuan. And it's his own doing. Not like Kar—eh, best to not think about her, after that nightmare.

Narcís has one major advantage, though: as my friend, he's exempt from the category of "fucking whale," which is what I call everybody with a BMI over 35.

In my mind only. I'm not so suicidal as to call them that to their faces. Some obese guys are surprisingly strong. Hot-tempered, too. Potential threats to the health of anyone who rashly reminds them of their condition.

Well, let them kill me—if they can catch me, because I can sure outrun them. But that doesn't change a basic fact: I'll never be like them. I'd rather die than let my body go.

No, I'm planning to retire someday and enjoy life.

I'm not making this up. To be a condomnaut, you don't necessarily have to be a muscle freak or a gymnast or an expert in martial arts, but you should be able to control your own body—especially the body parts that bodybuilders, gymnasts, and martial arts masters tend to neglect.

To be a condomnaut, you don't necessarily have to be a muscle freak or a gymnast or an expert in martial arts, but you should be able to control your own body—especially the body parts that body builders, gymnasts, and martial arts masters tend to neglect.

Nothing wrong with looking fantastic, of course.

"*¡Completo Camagüey!*" I pant, marking the end of my exercise routine with a Cuban phrase that must have already been ancient when I heard it from the grown-ups back in Rubble City, though I never really understood what it meant. "Listen, if you're all that impatient, why don't you play with Diosdadito for a while. Just leave me alone. I need a couple of minutes to take a shower and get dressed, and then we'll go. Bet I'll get there at practically the same time as everyone else, but unlike them I'll be . . . "

" . . . fresh and unstressed, right?" Narcís finishes my sentence for me. Then he smiles and raises his colossal right arm toward the ring of magnetic fields that runs around the entire perimeter of my apartment, a couple of inches from the ceiling. That's the energy cage of my biovort, Diosdadito. "You're a calculating scoundrel, Josué. You not just scheming to make Miquel think you're always ready for anything; you also don't want anyone to suspect you were tipped off due to my good ear and exceptional deductive abilities," he says with false modesty, while the approach of his biofield sends my pet scurrying to investigate, with a fabulous display of colors. "*Cojons*, I love your creature. What a pity you refuse to sell it to me—it's always so affectionate."

Sell it? Dream on. Not even to Narcís, my best friend.

That is, unless I have to face some catastrophe. Such as not having my contract renewed, which would make my economic situation go downhill, fast.

A biovort—short for biovortex—is a small creature composed of energy. Biovorts live in the coronas of a handful of rare stars in the Milky Way. Though not rational beings, they are among the very few plasma-based life forms, or lifelike forms, that exist. So their price is literally astronomical. So high that I never could have allowed myself to own one, except that a certain Kigran was so satisfied by my performance during Contact that she decided to give me an extra gift for my skill and dedication to interspecies fraternity. This was in spite of our brutal difference in size: her, more than three hundred meters long; me, just under five foot seven tall.

With my usual amalgam of nostalgia and guilt, I named my plasmic gift "Diosdadito" in honor of the old *babalawo* from my Rubble City childhood. It cost me an arm and a leg to set up a containment system inside my apartment to safely hold a creature that could vaporize the whole building in an instant if ionized gas were to escape from one of its magnetic branches. But the truth is, it really impresses my visitors, the way it darts across the ceiling and puts on spectacular shows of shifting shapes and colors. Too bad I can't pet it like Antares. All the same, it's proof of how well things are going for me. Quite the status symbol.

And it really helped me impress that materialist, Nerys.

Exobiologists tell me that some biovorts even come to recognize their owners. So I still have hopes that one of these years Diosdadito will stop offering its dazzling displays of pleasure to every stranger who pops by (even if it's a regular visitor, such as Nerys or Narcís and his wife Sonya) and reserve all or at least most of its affections for its master. What's the point of having a pet, whatever its price, if not only you're unable to touch it, but it's not even going to pay you any special attention?

"It definitely likes you, Narcís. One of these days I'm going to go crazy and, forget about selling it, I'll give it to you. But back to what we were saying: man, I still don't believe a bit of what you told me," I reply from the bathroom, pulling off my gym shorts.

I show off my muscles in the mirror, then run my fingers over my face, content. In spite of all the recent (and costly!) plastic surgery I've had done to get rid of my childhood scars from Rubble City (acne, insect bites), I'm still no Adonis. Especially not in Nu Barsa, one of the epicenters of beauty in the Human Sphere, where few people die without ever retouching the body and face that Mother Nature gave them.

But with these biceps and deltoids, which Yamil would have died for, and the dreadlocks I've been patiently cultivating for the past few years, at least nobody will call me "Zero" now.

Also, the light skin that drove me to despair in my childhood is perfectly normal here.

Yes, I've left all my childhood traumas behind. Except one. From which I make my living.

I step into the shower, leaving the door ajar so I can keep talking to Narcís—and keep enjoying my pet's amazing color show.

I turn on my sophisticated Tornado shower system, which immediately surrounds me with rotating jets, shooting ten times more water at my body in one minute than I could have consumed in a whole month in Rubble City.

Who cares if the water, like almost everything else in this enormous habitat, has been recycled a thousand times? Point is, I get to use as much as I want. And the massage feels so good. . . .

"What is it you don't believe?" Narcís asks from the living room.

I raise my voice in the midst of the aquatic storm to answer, "I don't believe you're going to retire, and I especially don't believe Aliens have finally appeared from beyond the Milky—"

"Shush, Josué!" paranoid Narcís whisper-shouts, scaring Diosdadito who frenetically pulsates purple and Prussian blue, transforming from its usual round shape into a sort of electric serpent, its demented angles zigzagging throughout the apartment at top speed. "In Nu Barsa, and in the home of a foreign condomnaut freelancer, the walls may have ears. Prudent Miquel doesn't even trust us Catalans; imagine someone like you! But, hey, would you really give it to me?" He watches Diosdadito thoughtfully, letting his breath out in a pachydermic sigh. "Forget it. If I brought it home, Sonya would scream to high heaven—and toss me into the street, no doubt about it. Apart from the expense of installing all this magnetic fencing, with our boys it would be like letting an atomic bomb wander around the ceiling." He shook his head and went on talking in his regular fat and happy baritone. "Well, it's true, friend. Believe it or not, I did resign. I hung up my saber. Quit the whole shebang. I'm not a Contact Specialist anymore. Shit, I'm forty-two years old and I have two boys, aged five and three, you know, whose mother still manages to tell them lies about what their father really does for a living, but the truth is, they barely recognize me when they see me."

It's true: some double standards refuse to die.

It's a tricky problem. There are still adults who haven't figured out how to tell their kids what exactly it is we condomnauts do that makes us so famous and important. It's especially hard when they're your own kids, and you're the guy who's famous for, you know, doing nobody-really-wants-to-say-what. For all our sex appeal to some, for all our fame and money, the fact is, there still aren't as many mixed marriages (between condomnaut and non-) as some people suppose.

And as for the kids—let's just say, I admire Narcís's tenacity. But I feel more certain every day that I'll never follow in his footsteps. I find it hard enough to justify what I do to myself.

Of course, I never say any of this out loud. Narcís is my friend. But I figure he knows it as well as I do.

"Yeah, Sonya's a saint," I agree, thinking about my friend's wife, as tiny and quiet as he is fat and outgoing, but equally headstrong. I switch the Tornado from thick streams of water to comforting jets of heated air, which have me warm and dry in an instant.

"She likes you, too, Josué—but she'll still never agree to keep your energy pet in our home." He brightens up and continues, radiating a sincere contentment that Diosdadito must be able to perceive clearly, because it glows a cheerful pink and green and returns to its spherical shape. "So I thought to myself, this business of waltzing all over the cosmos, willing and able to go to bed at any time with any Alien life form that might sell us some new appliance, was starting to feel like it wasn't what had fascinated me at first. Maybe the time had come for me to devote myself to being a normal father and raising my kids without shameful secrets coming between us. And since I've saved enough for my family to live on for a few years, until I can find another profession, I put in for retirement. And there I was, signing the papers—retinal patterns, fingerprint scans, DNA, all the forms of ID they require for you to get your pension—when suddenly there's all this excitement, everybody running around. I've never seen the office in such a state, or Impassive Miquel so animated. So I put two and two together, and started feeling as happy as a clam that it wasn't my problem anymore. Then I remembered my little Cuban friend and zipped straight over to give you the news. It was as clear as could be that this could only mean one thing. Oh, and congratulations, by the way! I heard how well you did on your last Contact. The Evita Entity, eh? It isn't every day you make Contact with a new telepathic, biotech, polymorph species."

"Thanks, not that I deserve it; it was sheer luck. And thanks for the tip, too, brother." I emerge from the bath completely dry, perfumed, and talcum-powdered, but still naked (an old joke with my friend, who loftily ignores my attempts to seduce his massive self), and pat Narcís on his back, as broad as a buffalo's.

At ceiling level, thrilled with our harmonious friendliness, Diosdadito has now become a rapidly spinning ring, pulsating between sky blue and baby-chick yellow. If it were a cat it would be purring, I suppose. "Do you think one of our ships found them?" I ask, suddenly worried, as I put on my lavender-blue underwear.

This color choice probably would have earned me a stoning in Rubble City. Funny how when I was a kid in the Caribbean, which became one of the pioneering regions on Earth for gay and bi as the dominant patterns of sexuality, machismo still clung stubbornly to an antiquated notion of strict heterosexualism. Just like Jordi—before he got mixed up with me, that is.

The biovort empathically picks up on the anxiety concealed behind my tone and turns olive green, taking on the vague shape of an anvil—not a bad imitation of a storm cloud.

"My guess is, it was much ado about nothing. Or maybe just a rowdy office party," Narcís reflects, trying to calm my pet and me at the same time.

Pleased, I open my wardrobe and after a moment's hesitation tug on a lavender-blue shirt and a spider-silk smartsuit, then put on a pair of autoadaptable shoes of Sirian dolphin leather (Sirius: Radian 167, Quadrant 14; best leather in the galaxy; too bad the Kigrans exploit it). My outfit is worth more than all of Rubble City put together.

In this getup, and with only my Countdown collar for jewelry, nobody will mistake me for anything but what I am. Why hide it? Lots of people imitate us; in Nu Barsa, and throughout the Human Sphere, we Contact Specialists are the trendsetters, like movie stars and musicians used to be.

"Just another wild goose chase, then. The gazillionth." I breathe easier, closing my eyes, the better to luxuriate in the delicious sensation of sophisticated fabrics and expensive footwear adapting themselves millimeter by millimeter to my exact shape. Now I'm the one who'd be purring if he could. "Probably somebody saw, or thought they saw, yet again, the phantom extragalactic Aliens, or found traces of them, but they still haven't made Contact. So I could still be a hero for Nu Barsa if I pull it off."

"Bravo for your spirit, Cubanito. But that may not be so easy." Narcís's qualms bring me down again. "I thought I heard the word 'Qhigarians.' If those polymorphic hoodwinking hobos are in on this . . ."

I tremble, just thinking of what that might possibly mean. Diosdadito blazes red and violet on the ceiling, reflecting my worries.

But no. Think positive. That's another essential for being a good condomnaut. With an almost physical effort, I push all thoughts about the asshole Alien Drifters and their thousands of shapes and worldships out of my head. I manage to crack a reasonably nonchalant smile, and my sensitive biovort dials its color back to pure sky blue.

"You must have misheard," I speculate, standing at my apartment's door. "Anyway, however it turns out, I'll cross that bridge when I come to it."

"*We'll* cross it, Josué. *We* will cross it," Narcís says emphatically, waddling over after saying goodbye to my pet, who glows a happy red. If it were a dog, I'm sure it would be wagging its tail now. Its lack of selectivity is so inappropriate for a companion animal. Especially such an expensive one.

Maybe I should find myself a cat, like Antares.

"I thought you said you just retired," I tease. Locking the DNA-controlled door behind us, we step onto the slow, narrow moving pathway that takes us to the much faster moving hallway outside.

"Did you think Cheapskate Miquel would let me go, just like that?" My enormous friend shrugs comically, and, as we are in a bit of a rush, we walk at a brisk pace on the building's internal transport system, which does barely two kilometers an hour through the wide vestibule. "I had to make a couple of concessions, buddy. But I came out ahead: I'll still be working for the powerful Department of Contacts, except I'll be a consultant. And for this mission, I'm afraid they're going to need all my experience and advice."

A teenager from the second floor steps out of the elevator, recognizes me, and (staring at my outfit, a cheap imitation of which he will wear tomorrow to impress his friends) calls me by first name.

I don't respond, just as I didn't respond to Narcís, but not because I'm playing the big star.

I'm simply concentrating on the semiacrobatic feat of stepping quickly from the building's slow walkway to the outer belt of the public Rambla Móvil, which does five kilometers an hour, an average pedestrian's speed.

A great invention, these moving sidewalks, though people always complain the maintenance costs a fortune. But at least in this exclusive residential neighborhood, Ensanche Nuovo, one of the most expensive in Nu Barsa, they run like clockwork.

Narcís and I advance almost mechanically, with scarcely a second between transitions, from the outer belt to the innermost ones on the Rambla Móvil. Each belt runs five kilometers an hour faster than the last. The last one, in the center, moves at a respectable fifty kilometers an hour, with double grab rails on posts every four meters. We find one to hold on to, just in case, and in less than two minutes we reach the maglev monorail terminal. Hardly moving a muscle. Viva New Barcelona. Viva la technology.

Narcís and I wait silently on the maglev platform for the next car to arrive. Just takes ninety seconds. It isn't rush hour; it's never rush hour in the enclave, especially not in Ensanche Nuovo. The artificial sun above the enclave goes through a twenty-four-hour brightness cycle, but it never turns off, and good planning has divided the habitat's population into three shifts for work and time off.

We get on and, as we're the only passengers on the sleek, swift car, we take advantage of one of our privileges as Contact

Specialists to key in a top priority destination, turning the already fast public transportation system into our own private superexpress train.

Having no need now to turn aside or stop at any other platforms, the AI controlling the maglev readily accelerates and after a few hundred meters hits eight hundred kilometers an hour. Not its top velocity, just normal cruising speed. We're in a rush, but it's no emergency.

The car has no windows. Enormous panoramic holoscreens equipped with dizziness filters allow us to enjoy the outside view perfectly well, without running the risk of motion sickness from looking directly at the blurred landscape rushing past.

As in old Barcelona on Earth, here, too, the Catalans have built an enviable transportation network. This organizing business comes easily to them, almost like with the Germans, I'm told.

Hopefully I'll get to visit Neue Heimat someday and find out for myself. See if that conceited ass Jürgen Schmodt wasn't exaggerating when he bragged about his home planet.

Our destination, the Central del Govern, administrative heart of Nu Barsa, is a dense cluster of towers (red and gold, of course: Viva Catalonia!) visible in the distance. So tall that, if it were on Earth, Gaudí's original Sagrada Familia would look like a chunky stump next to them.

In fact, the complex includes a replica of the great basilica that once symbolized historic Barcelona. Twice the original size, yet still dwarfed by its sleek descendants.

Catalans feel such reverence for their brilliant Catholic architect, there must be at least six replicas of Park Güell in Nu Barsa.
And I've counted like fifteen Casas de la Pedrera. Not to mention
the hyperjump frigate I serve on, named after him. I wouldn't
be surprised if any day now they present the New Vatican with
a petition to beatify and canonize him. If they haven't done so
already. Saint Gaudí—got a ring to it, you know.

The lightweight, highly resistant carbon-tubule internal struc-
tures of these graceful gold and scarlet towers (heraldic colors
of the historical Counts of Barcelona), plus the Algolese gravitic
systems that control them, allow them to rise as high as ten kilometers in some areas. The skeletal buildings are interconnected
by countless bridges and walkways, like an elegant oversized
tribute to the Metropolis of twentieth-century director Fritz
Lang's visionary film.

It's such an impressive sight, I sometimes forget that Nu
Barsa, like most human colonies beyond the Solar System, isn't
an authentic planet but an artificial habitat.

In other words, a space station. But what a station!

Neither Konstantin Tsiolkovsky, nor Robert Goddard, nor Lynn
Poole, nor Wernher Von Braun, nor Arthur C. Clarke, nor any
of the other daring pioneers of astronautics or of science fiction
who fantasized wildly in the twentieth century, imagining orbital
rings, excavated asteroids, and a variety of other permanent human
habitats in space, ever conceived of a structure this immense.

I savor once more the magnificence of the spectacle. There's
a reason it's so expensive to live here.

The small asteroids containing the force field and the artificial sun, a triad of barely visible black spots at the zenith, surrounding the constant fusion blaze of our "pocket star," are exactly fifty kilometers up in the sky.

Not technically sky, but whatever. What matters is that the volume under the "roof" is not only big enough to holoproject a full sky but for genuine water vapor clouds to form and float overhead, along with helicopters, turbocopters, gravimobiles, and all sorts of aerial vehicles, and plenty of room to spare.

The "ground" is a simple layer, two or three meters thick, of organic topsoil over an expansive force field that knits together the dozen or so small asteroids containing the generators. All Algolese technology. We use it even though we don't understand the mathematics behind it, and our physicists swear up and down that no Unified Field Theory is possible.

Well, our physicists haven't exactly been the most brilliant ones in the universe lately. We treat Algolese "gravitic witchcraft" pretty much like we do the Taraplin hyperengines that the Qhigarians sell us: nobody is dumb enough not to use it just because we can't understand it.

From edge to edge, the huge Catalan orbital enclave measures almost five hundred kilometers across. So, using the simple formula for the area of a circle, pi times the radius squared, that makes . . .

How much? I'm not up to doing it in my head, and I don't feel like distracting the monorail's AI with trivia. Let's say, about two hundred thousand square kilometers. That's the figure the authorities on this gigantic archology always bandy about when they're showing it off to their generally stunned visitors.

Perfect Caribbean dimensions. Somewhat larger than my own native island, or a little smaller than all the Antilles put together.

A real space island, floating in one of the Lagrange points around Pi y Margall, a yellow dwarf in Radian 457, Quadrant 12, invisible from Earth and with only three planets—all gas giants with no satellites, and therefore absolutely inappropriate for colonization. That's the only reason the greedy Arctians allowed us to occupy this system for a modest sum, and even let us rename its primary after the Catalan statesman, even though it lies well within their sphere of influence.

Zipping over on the monorail, the only thing that reminds us we're on a man-made orbital habitat and not a planet is the uncanny flatness of the horizon.

Nu Barsa isn't the largest human orbital enclave; that would be Commonwealth, belonging to the Anglo-Indo-Australo-Jamaicans, which orbits Bannard, a star much closer to Earth. It measures 750 kilometers in diameter and has seventy kilometers of "sky with atmosphere" from ground to zenith.

Once again I reflect that, while we humans may have conquered space thanks to the Aliens, especially the extinct Taraplins, their generous Qhigarian heirs, and their marvelous hyperengines, it's also true (and I can't help but feel proud at the thought) that we couldn't have done it without the selfless hard work of Contact Specialists such as Narcís and myself.

No technology available to humanity in the twenty-second century would have made it possible for us to construct a space archology as enormous and as distant from the Solar System as this one—or, for that matter, even to transport the eleven million Catalans and the four million representatives of other nationalities who live here today. Especially not in such short order.

Thank goodness for Algolese gravity tech. And Arctian high-efficiency biorecycling systems and many more Alien technologies, without which humanity might be nothing but a sad memory today, just another line on the long galactic list of extinct civilizations, starting with the Taraplins. A list dutifully maintained by their Qhigarian heirs.

Likewise, the Russians, Canadians, Brazilians, South Africans, Japanese, and Germans—the only nations that have managed to either buy (at very steep prices) or discover and then occupy planets that are more or less terraformable—could never have reached their new and very distant worlds of Rodina, New Thule, Nova Saudade, Krugerland, Amaterasu, and Neue Heimat, were it not for the Taraplin-designed hyperjump engines sold by those same Qhigarians.

Well. Narcís fell asleep. Par for the course when he rides the monorail. And now he's snoring up a storm.

I, for my part, am staring absentmindedly at the panoramic holoscreen, watching woodlands, towns, lakes, and fields stream past. It almost seems natural to think about travel when you're moving this fast through a habitat as impressive as Nu Barsa.

After an impasse that lasted nearly a century and a half (due to the Five Minute War, among other things), the second and most dazzling stage of the human adventure in space began. It got started by sheer chance, as is often the case. One fortunate day, May 19, 2154, the distinguished Catalan astronaut Joaquim Molá was on a one-man exploratory mission for the European Union, looking for water-ice comets in the Oort cloud, when he made First Contact with an Alien species.

Or it might be more accurate to say that it all started when the wily Quim got the first twenty-five hyperjump engines ever acquired by humanity from the Qhigarians in exchange for nothing more than his cat and a Catalan–Spanish–English dictionary. (The cat, by the way, was named Aldebaran, according to his log; apparently it was already a custom back them to give Arabic star names to the cats that ships kept as pets and mascots.) This was probably the most profitable and providential trade anyone's heard of since the Dutch bought Manhattan from the Indians for twenty-two dollars.

Nobody denies that cats are the best mascots a ship could have, as Antares reminds me every time I travel. So maybe the Qhigarians didn't make such a bad deal in the long run. Not to mention that the Catalan–Spanish–English diction-ary must have been a real gem for them; they're completely obsessed with learning new languages. They're still trying to talk us into selling them our most current translation software. No deal, of course: that is our main trump card for making Contact.

Still, every time I think about that episode, I don't know why, but it brings to mind that old joke about how copper wire was invented: two Catalans picked up a one-peseta coin at the same time, and they each tugged on it, both refusing to let go.

Molá was a sharp negotiator and a hero for all humanity, yet he is nonetheless despised as nearly a traitor and a flaming idiot, both in the reduced remnant of old Catalonia on Earth and in this flourishing Catalan enclave of Nu Barsa.

I can understand. Every self-respecting Catalan must get angry at the thought that their fellow countryman could have kept them all of those precious hyperengines for his own people instead of giving (not even selling!) twenty of them to the rest of humanity. Then they'd probably be living on an entire planet of their own, New Catalonia, and not this orbital habitat. Sure, it's a big habitat, but pitifully limited.

The rest of the human race would have had to pay the Catalans for the rights to use the Taraplin-Qhigarian hyperengine, just as now they pay the Russians for the high-efficiency biorecyclers they got from the Arctians. Otherwise, fuck them.

Whether or not Quim Molá was a traitor, we humans were very lucky.

In what had looked like our darkest hour—not long after the terrible Five Minute War between China and North America in 2136, with the consequent radioactive contamination, entire cities completely wiped out or partially destroyed (including Madrid and Barcelona, by the way), and even worse, the catastrophic climate change that followed, with floods and droughts unleashing the worst famine in history and reducing the swarming population of seven billion in less than a decade to a scant, starving nine hundred million—just when it seemed like a Solar System with no colonizable planets would be our grave, the Aliens and their new technologies opened up the Galaxy to us.

And today, almost five decades later, on the brink of the twenty-third century, if we play our cards right, other Aliens—this time, extragalactic—may open up the entire Universe.

The maglev car begins to decelerate. Too soon, it seems. The heart of the city, the Central del Govern, which old Catalans prefer to call El Govern, the complex of tall buildings from which Nu Barsa is run, is just beginning to come into focus, still kilometers away.

"Impressive, isn't it, Josué?" The change of velocity wakes Narcís, who guesses what I'm thinking. Not too hard to do, as I'm staring at the majestic spectacle of the distant stylized towers and suspension bridges we're heading for.

The labyrinthine yet elegant Central buildings defy the artificial gravity generated underneath the enclave, spreading their almost calligraphic filigree across woodlands, fields, rivers, even lakes. Narcís gazes at them and sighs, contented. "Every time I ask myself why the devil I have so many more Alien than human females on my list of sexual partners, I look at all this and, knowing it's our home because of people like me, I feel . . . let's say, rewarded." He yawns, settling comfortably on the wide double seat of the maglev car, which his monumental backside fills almost entirely.

Once more he's managed to make his words sound as they're imbued with a genuine spirit of sacrifice. Well, after all, he may really feel that way.

So all I say is, "Yes, it's a lovely habitat. Hopefully I'll soon be one of its proud and happy citizens." And I hold back the rest of my comments.

A second later my friend is snoring again, placid as an angel.

I watch him. It's funny: every time I try to imagine this adipose mass, Narcís, having sexual relations with any living creature, whether it's an Alien female or his own heroic wife, my brain simply blocks me.

His remarkable success as a condomnaut is the greatest mystery in the Department of Contacts. He takes the job with such a quiet sense of duty, it simply leaves no room for anything else. Libido during Contact? Don't even dream of it. Asexual Narcís, some sardonically call him. Behind his back, of course. You don't make a joke like that to the face of someone who weighs in at 300 kilos, even if it's not exactly all muscle.

The gossips also speculate, half as a joke and half seriously, that Narcís Puigcorbé owes the many profitable trade deals he's achieved in the course of his brilliant career to the fact that the Alien Contact Specialists wanted to recognize his boundless goodwill, or that they felt sorry for his incompetence as a lover. Or both.

Because as to being a good person, few are in his league. In the orgasm department, however, most doubt that he even felt one when he fathered his children with his wife. Much less gave her one.

To be sure, one of those mocking skeptics—I'm almost ashamed to admit this—is me. Perhaps because he's never propositioned me, or reacted to my subtle provocations.

Well, let's not exaggerate. I'm even ready to accept that he and Sonya must enjoy it, at least a little, because they have two sons. Besides, if they didn't . . .

Thing is, without sexual pleasure, however twisted it may be, our profession is simply unimaginable.

I'm standing as I've done so often and watching the fake Montjuïc in the distance. One of these days I really should get myself together and go there. I've been saying this for years. It's a fairly faithful copy of the original. Barcelona was defined, before the Five Minute War, as a city lying between the sea and the mountain. But it would have been too expensive and fruitless to try and create a convincing replica of the Mediterranean in the enclave. Farmland and pastureland, which alternate like a patchwork quilt in the distance, were much more necessary. You can't feed fifteen million inhabitants on nothing but hydroponics. Not to mention that the weight of so much water on the force field under the "ground" might have overtaxed the gravity generators, Algolese tech and all.

The best deal that nostalgic environmentalists could cut with the engineers, cattle raisers, and farmers was to install the beautiful string of ponds I see stretching to the horizon.

To be sure, they're teeming with edible fish. Catalans sure know how to squeeze every last drop of economic juice out of each little detail, even if it seems merely decorative.

Must be in their genes.

Whether or not his fellow Catalans despise him, I've always thought that Joaquim Molá was not only a good negotiator but a quick mind for grasping new situations, an imaginative improviser, and, fortunately, someone with few moral scruples, too.

Or a sexual pervert of such magnitude that he makes all of his enterprising heirs in the Nu Barsa Department of Contacts look tiny, regardless of which generation we are lumped with. Though it seems the Qhigarians on the ship with which Quim made Contact weren't terribly different from us humans.

They had two arms and two legs, at any rate, and when you're dealing with Contacts, that's saying a lot.

Molá was also smart enough that, on his triumphant return to Earth minus one cat and one dictionary, but with the addition of the first twenty-five Taraplin hyperengines from the Qhigarians safely stowed in his storage room, he abstained from telling every last detail about the trade meeting in which he had obtained them.

It was only later on, when we were spreading out across space thanks to thousands of those engines, purchased one by one from the "generous" Qhigarians, and humanity was beginning to have more frequent and necessarily closer relations with the Galactic Community, that it became clear how Molá had sealed the deal with those first Qhigarians by . . .

The journalists of the day, as fond of euphemisms as they were of scandals, referred to it as "sleeping with" a crew member from the Alien ship.

Asked about it shortly thereafter by a famous satirical weekly, Molá said only that it hadn't been all that difficult: a female's a female, he told them, Qhigarian or human, and of course he had used a condom!

Many believe that the colloquial term for my trade comes from that brief admission by Quim.

Bad joke, right?

Well, just think of it as theory number 23,456 about the origin of our name. As valid as any of the previous 23,455 theories, in my humble opinion.

And as many more new theories have been thrown out since that time, you know.

The Protocol for First Contact has nothing to say about condoms or other such crudely physical protective barriers or filters.

The number of intelligent species found in the Milky Way comes to twenty-nine thousand so far. That is if we count the wide variety of beings that live on the Qhigarian worldships as belonging to a single species, contrary to the opinions of skeptical exobiologists. Otherwise the total would nearly double.

So if you bear in mind that the list continues to grow by several dozen new species a year (and the older species tell us, with relief, that centuries ago new Contacts numbered in the hundreds per year), such as my newfound Evita Entity, as well as that most of these new civilizations also set off to explore the galaxy in new directions, it's easy to understand that finding ships, planets, colonies, or representatives of other intelligent species has come to be as unremarkable an event as meeting a neighbor on the moving walkway.

The importance of allowing the accepted norms to regulate such encounters should be obvious.

Much more ancient than humanity, and supposedly Taraplin in origin (since the Qhigarians insist that they inherited this curious custom from their mentors), the odd interspecies etiquette known as the Protocol for First Contact has been well received by almost all the sentient species in the Milky Way.

Briefly stated, here's how it works: if you meet the representatives of an Alien species off in space for the first time—and if you want to make your peaceful intentions clear, in case some mutually advantageous trading might take place between your two kinds at some future date, as opposed to immediate mutual destruction—you show them that you decline to consider them Aliens, at least for a while.

In other words, you happily "sleep" with them. Or at least pretend you're doing it happily. Even if afterward, paradoxically, you can't sleep for days just thinking about it.

On the other hand, if you already know them and you want something from them, that's simply a Contact, not a First Contact. That makes matters even simpler: whether it's information, technology, merchandise, or anything else they have that you want, first you negotiate the deal, pay them with something they want—and then, you guessed it: it really helps keep the exchange flowing if you show them one more time that, at least for a while, you will cease to consider them Aliens. So in the name of goodwill and better trade relations present and future, you "sleep" with them, happily or not. Preferably while staying as wide awake as possible.

There's obviously no rule against using nonbiological protective barriers; sometimes you have no choice but to turn to them, such as when your oxygen-based body has to get together with a fluorine-based life form. But aside from such extreme cases, anything as crude as a physical barrier or filter such as a condom is generally considered an unpleasant discourtesy, as well as evidence of the underdeveloped medical sciences in the culture whose representatives resort to such crude measures.

The Countdown, which only protects the integrity of your DNA, doesn't count. Nor do immune system boosters or antiviral vaccines.

Which is good, because even with their use there have been more than a few condomnauts who've died in strict quarantine after coming down with strange sexually transmitted diseases, if that's the right term for them. This was especially true during the early years of enthusiastic Contacts with the Galactic Community, before our immunologists were forced to become as expert as those of most other Alien species.

The leaders of the dozens of clashing factions into which the decimated human population of the twenty-second century was divided after the Five Minute War soon realized that the Protocol for Contacts, whether Taraplin in origin or not, made it so that the species with better command of biology would almost always gain the lion's share in any trade. Oxygen-based life forms who could "naturally" modify not only their anatomy but their body chemistry would have an indisputable advantage over others with less advanced biotech when it came to making Contact with, for example, a new race of methane breathers.

And forget about the even more exotic yet perfectly real cases, such as the arachnoids of Vulpecula IV, whose chemistry is based not on carbon but on the exotic element germanium.

Well! After the initial wave of enthusiasm about Molá's lucky trade, things were starting to look rather gloomy for us. If we wanted to sail through the cosmos, we'd have to make Contact. But who could get excited about seeing a Vulpian arachnoid with its rare toxic metabolism? Or for that matter, even an amphibious newt from Wurplheos VII, with its profusion of spiny fins and pink and green polka-dotted skin?

What astronaut could be asked to make such a sacrifice, after years of painstaking study of technical science?

But everybody knows we're a lucky species. It turned out we already had people who were not only capable of facing such bizarre Contacts, but even of enjoying them. Us.

People who had for countless centuries been shamefully rejected as perverts or sexual deviants. Gays, bisexuals, masochists, sadists and fetishists, the odd and the aberrational, the more or less satisfied victims of unspeakable paraphilias, we who had once been confined to madhouses or jails, or even executed to keep the moral cancer that infected us from contaminating the horrified "sexually healthy" members of society.

But as you know, everything is relative in the Lord's vineyard. Morality depends on convenience; after news of the more salacious details about Quim Molá's First Contact with the Qhigarians had gotten around (though various governments tried to keep them a secret), there was a strange, radical, and absolutely unexpected inversion in sexual values. Practically overnight, we, the same black sheep that the community had refused for millennia to consider members with full rights, had become important, essential, indispensable. The prosperity of the entire human race depended in large measure not only on our negotiating skill but, even more important, on what society used to consider sexual deviancy and sin.

What irony: from pariahs to heroes, just like that.

Well, not just like that. Things didn't shift right away right then, either, to tell the truth.

But it sure did help.

Indeed, a wave of sexual liberation began that continues to this day. Any upright citizen of the twentieth or twenty-first century would probably be horrified by our contemporary society, in which heterosexuality is only one possibility among many, not at all the majority or "correct" orientation that it was assumed to be for so many years.

Conscious of our historic mission, reveling in all sorts of dirty space fantasies in our twisted minds, we who once were shunned and stigmatized for our divergent sexuality now march with chests puffed in pride, aiming for the stars. The same mass of humanity who for so long spit on us, rejected us, denounced, repudiated, and killed us, now see us off with cheers and fanfare as their new (sexual) ambassadors. And they imitate us—to the degree that they can.

I guess they think that if "sleeping" with strange creatures is the way to conquer the stars; then why not sleep around! Starting with our own kind, just for practice.

The new foreign policy, and the morality derived from it, had many detractors at first, of course. Just about every religion in sight screamed to high heaven against "space immorality" and declared it would be a thousand times more preferable to languish and die "pure" on Earth without access to sophisticated Alien technology than to survive and conquer the stars at such a repugnant price.

The imams called for a space jihad. From the Vatican, neo-Pope Innocence XXIV issued an irate encyclical accusing Contact Specialists of being heirs to Sodom and Gomorrah, mocking God, and worshiping lewd demons from the depths of space. He excommunicated them all, scornfully terming them "condomnauts," never suspecting that this would become the popular nickname for the new and prestigious profession.

Yes, that's theory number 23,457. Didn't I warn you there'd be more?

Save me the details about all the others, please.

But it backfired on His Holiness. And they talk about papal infallibility.

In any case, it is worth noting that the next occupant of the throne of Saint Peter, John XXVIII, not only withdrew the irate excommunication that his predecessor had hastily launched against us, but even transferred the Holy See of the Roman Catholic Church to outer space. Precisely, to the orbital enclave known as Novo Vaticano, built with Alien technology (of course) in orbit around Beta Crucis in the Southern Cross.

That's what's I call poetic justice. Or opportunistic repentance. Or, don't spit into the wind.

It quickly became clear that the human race had truly lucked out with Quim Molá, because not all sexual perverts work out as condomnauts. Not at all.

Unfortunately, attitude alone isn't enough. It also takes some aptitude.

Some species in the Galactic Community are more Alien to us than others. For example, "sleeping" with an Algolese woman, despite her height (two meters tall), her green hair, her violet skin, her mouth full of yellowish canines, and her language replete with ultrasonic frequencies that make your hair stand on end, is almost like a walk in the park for most human condomnauts.

Indeed, considering that both our species evolved from primates (or the equivalent), it almost seems like making love with a distant cousin. Plus, the voluntary control that the females of Algol have over the musculature of their vaginas is quite the extra added attraction for making Contact with them.

Little wonder that the second Alien technology that humanity acquired was none other than the gravitic control developed by these distant cousins.

On the other hand, making Contact with a rorqual from Kigrai (that is, Ophiuchus), with a body hundreds of meters long and three vaginas, each of them several meters wide and smelling of salted fish gone bad—that's quite a feat!

I honestly wish sometimes there were more rational hermaphrodite species in the galaxy. Or at least with less recognizable sexual organs.

But sadly, even in the vast reaches of space, things are never so weird that they don't remind you of something from back home. And sometimes it's something you wish you'd never seen back home.

Do I ever know it. It's been years, and I still have the occasional nightmare. Though I got Diosdado out of the deal.

And since quality generally comes at a high price, it turns out that whereas Algolese are, as a species, almost as young and devoid of sophisticated technologies as we are (and I emphasize that "almost," in a place like this, which exists only due to Algolese gravity controls), the gigantic Kigrans are among the most powerful species in the Galactic Community. They're hoarding more valuable biotech inventions than ten or twelve other races put together.

Secrets that lots of us would love to get our hands on, such as their bioships, their genetically individualized drugs, their biobatteries, their controlled cellular regeneration . . .

So there's always a call for more and better condomnauts.

It was soon determined that, apart from exceptional cases such as Contact with the Furasgans, who are intelligent only when young and lose the ability to reason as they grow, or Termizarian reptiloids, who only practice heterosexual sex for reproduction and the rest of the time are happily homoerotic, pedophiles and pederasts are rarely suited to the task. Their spectrum of preferences tends to be simply too narrow.

Fetishists, however, such as furries, who are obsessed with dressing up as animals in plush costumes, and especially zoophiles, who love sex with animals, have found making Contact with Aliens to be the profession of *our* dreams.

Dreams some of us have, anyway. Or nightmares. Depends on how you look at it.

It also became obvious pretty quickly that, despite the publicity being given to this amazing new job, there weren't enough pioneers with sufficient talent to get it done. Because being a pervert and ready for anything isn't enough, not by a long shot. You also have to grasp the basics of the art of negotiation and diplomacy, and have some notion of linguistics and cultural relativism, technology and science, social intuition, courtesy, tact—lots of skills, in other words.

And none of the governments ruling the motley mosaic of cultures among which the human survivors of the Five Minute War were still divided wanted to fall behind, especially once it became clear that after an Alien species trades technology with a species making Contact, the recipients are not deemed morally obliged to share the information they acquire with the rest of their kind. First the Russians, then the Canadians, then the Japanese, and so on, until all the most powerful nations, one after another, embarked on a race to create costly and well-equipped special schools that detected and groomed their self-sacrificing students for all sorts of inclinations—furry, zoophile, and everything else considered useful for Contact. And of course they trained their most talented students in the difficult ancient art of negotiation.

That led to such academies as Feather, Hide, and Scale in Nueva Madrid, and Pan-Galac Zoo in Karlovy-MheschePlakneta, and many more. Mothers from the lower classes (and some from not so low) brought and continue to bring their children to them, dreaming they may pass the nearly impossible admission exams and, after difficult and exhausting training sessions that too often even damage the students' mental health, acquire the professional education needed for travel into space as glorious Contact Specialists, ready to do anything as representatives of humanity to other races and cultures, navigating among the stars.

And most important of all, hoping they'll come back wealthy from the bonuses paid for making a successful Contact.

Of course, there weren't any expensive specialized schools operating in Rubble City, or in CH generally, or anywhere else in Cuba or the entire Caribbean, for that matter. So I broke into the trade in the hardest way possible: by improvising.

When Abel's hacking skills and his kindly nature provided me the money for a shuttle ticket to the Clifford Simak

Geosynchronic Transit Station (named in honor of a famous science fiction writer from the twentieth century, incidentally), the biggest duty-free habitat in orbit around Earth, it only took me a couple of hours to get a contract as a condomnaut with Agustí Palol, the captain of a small independent trading vessel flying under the Catalan flag. That was the hyperjump corvette *Juan de la Cierva*, which was preparing to take off with a crew of four, not on a heroic voyage of exploration to the depths of space or anything of the kind, but on its umpteenth routine trading journey around the so-called Zodiac Circuit.

Now, I didn't pick this corvette completely by chance; the history of technology and inventors has fascinated me since I was little, and I thought flying in a ship named after the brilliant Spanish inventor of the autogyro would bring me good luck. And so it did.

In theory, every human ship should carry a Contact Specialist on board, just in case it happens to be lucky enough to get involved in a First Contact with some new Alien race (as the odds say it will, sooner or later). Besides, according to the famous Protocol that the Qhigarians, as faithful disciples of the Taraplins, are determined to spread everywhere, it's supposed to be basically impossible to conduct any sort of trade unless a condomnaut is present to represent every species involved.

But in practice, many ships (and not only the human ones) risk navigating through the Milky Way without a Contact Specialist. This limits them to trading with already familiar merchants. Because, obviously, you don't need a condomnaut to trade hardware for fissionable material with humans from another enclave. Though some wish that was how it worked, if only it were limited to trade among ourselves.

But keeping up galactic standards for interspecies relations doesn't mean we have to do the same with our own. Besides, it would be too much work. Contact Specialists, human or otherwise, don't grow on trees. And normal individuals of most species aren't exactly willing to take part in effusive sexual intercourse with the representatives of other species, no matter how similar they look.

Sexual xenophobia isn't exclusive to Homo sapiens by any means. This is the particular irony of the Protocol that the Taraplins created: if everybody enjoyed making Contact, what sense would it make to become a condomnaut?

Of course there's always room for improvisation and even for professional impersonation; among us humans, and I suppose among some other Alien races as well, every once in a while an unscrupulous (and/or desperate) crew member will attempt to assume the prestigious role of Contact Specialist.

Impersonating a condomnaut is sort of like the last card in the deck for an astronaut who, for whatever reason, has lost or been abandoned by his ship, and who can't get any other space vehicle to hire them in any capacity. A desperate last resort, if you haven't got the training, or the stomach, for it. Some call it playing sexual roulette: if you're very lucky, you won't have to make Contact with anyone during the voyage; with a little less luck, it'll be something not totally disgusting, such as "sleeping" with an Algolese female; but if things go bad, you might always end up with a Kigran rorqual.

But even in that case, it'll go much better for the impostor who at least bites the bullet and gives it a try. According to the sacrosanct Contact Protocol of the Taraplins, if a hired condomnaut does not adequately perform his role as sexual ambassador in the way expected of him, the ship's captain has a perfect right not only to refuse to pay him what was promised, but even to launch him into deep space on the spot, as a fraud.

That's why more than a few impromptu Contact Specialists have gone insane (or at least have pretended to go insane) after stubbornly and desperately attempting to overcome their natural repugnance and make Contact with some particularly repulsive Alien. Just so they won't be abandoned in the middle of outer space by their disappointed and infuriated captains.

Well, nobody said our profession was always pleasant or free from danger.

Under these risky conditions I signed up with Captain Palol. I imagine that in spite of my swearing up and down that I had plenty of experience, he never believed me to be anything other than one more runaway teen, or at most a crew member who'd been left behind, perhaps an unlucky cabin boy. And he decided to give me a chance.

May the orishas bless his good heart.

And his gratitude for the good time I gave him in his office when he hired me . . .

After all, on its last twenty voyages, the corvette *Juan de la Cierva* had only come across the usual old friends: the Aliens from the so-called Ekhumen Merchanttil of Aries; the *sidhar* Iar Fjhoi and its people, bipeds with two arms and two eyes who could pass pretty easily for human on a dark night—if it weren't for their slight scent of hydrogen sulfide, their navy blue skin, the small horns over their eyes, and their short, scaly tails, that is.

But luck was on my side: on the return trip, after an utterly routine commercial exchange with Arietian merchants (three tons of quartz geodes from Earth, swapped for a ton and a half of Furasgan-manufactured ceramic hyperconductors; I suspect it was contraband of some sort, to come so cheap), our small Catalan-flagged merchant ship detected the exhaust of a sub-light speed space vehicle in the direction of the constellation Pisces.

Captain Agustí gave me a dubious look and asked, "Do you dare, Josué?" I nodded, though I was trembling like a leaf. I had them shoot me up with all the vaccines and immune boosters I could take without bursting, put on the Countdown collar, and, well, that's how humanity in general and the Catalans in particular made First Contact with the Continentines: gigantic masses of intelligent protoplasm from a double star system near the Hercules Globular Cluster. Confident of their physical endurance and biological immortality, after listening for thousands of years to radio transmissions from the Galactic Community, they had finally decided to set out for space—in ships propelled by nuclear fusion engines, no less!

That's what I call being in no hurry to get anywhere in particular. Good thing they get around now with Taraplin hyperengines. Thanks to Captain Palol and me.

My Contact with the gigantic hermaphrodite amoebas was one for the textbooks; in fact, it's already studied in a couple of academies. And I gained a lot of prestige. I admit that, speaking only for myself, entering a sea of cytoplasm protected only by a thin biosuit and swimming wherever the sol-gel changes led me isn't all that arousing. But apparently I really did have some natural talent for the job: the way I stimulated the immense cell's micronucleus proved so pleasurable for their Contact Specialist, they didn't hesitate before giving us—no charge!—nothing less than the secret to their cold fusion method. With that, I secured a practically limitless source of clean, cheap energy for Nu Barsa and became a real hero among the Catalans, who offered me a long-term contract at the princely salary I've been living on ever since in Ensanche Nuovo.

Over the past eight years, through ups and downs, I've covered half the galaxy aboard all sorts of hyperjump ships, from small corvettes to enormous cruisers, "sleeping" with dozens of Alien life forms on my Catalan employers' dime. Including eleven First Contacts.

And all that with no repercussions more troublesome than a fungoid rash I got from an infected Guzoid polyp. Nothing human pharmacology couldn't deal with, luckily. A bit of interferon and the Alien spores surrendered en masse to my strengthened immune system.

Not bad for a starving runaway brat from Rubble City, eh?

The maglev car starts picking up speed again. Apparently it didn't slow down a minute ago because we were arriving at our destination but just to let higher priority train pass.

At this point, accelerating is hardly worthwhile, though. We're practically in the shadow of the outer ring of thin towers that make up the Central del Govern.

Up at the top of the holoscreen I can see the unmistakable profile of the Department of Contacts building. I wish I had met the architect who designed it. Xavier Pugat must have had a sarcastic sense of humor. Back in the day people often said that skyscrapers, so tall and narrow, were simply crude phallic symbols. He did them one better, deciding that the edifice housing the Department of Contacts and all its Specialists should be precisely an enormous hyperrealistic phallus.

Makes sense, doesn't it?

He didn't even leave out the veins, and there's no mistaking the coloration. You almost expect to see a colossal, opalescent drop of semen emerging from the tip, which actually is the access to the central elevator and ventilation shafts.

"And here we are," Mateo puffs, stretching his monumental bulk so brusquely that the seat creaks as if in pain. "Back to the madhouse," he says with a beatific, or perhaps mischievous, smile. "Why the long face, Josué? Were you smoking wildwall, or is it that you don't want to go see Nerys and tell her all the details about your Contact with the Evita Entity?"

I let out my breath, imagining the mermaid's jealous reaction. "What's done is done. I'll take my lumps. The life of a Contact Specialist is a life of many sacrifices. Same goes for his girlfriend. In fact, I was thinking of visiting her today and telling her the whole story, with all the gory details. What's really eating me is the idea of seeing the chassis of that nanoborg, Herr Schmodt. Think he'll be there?"

"Hate to say it, but I *know* he's there." My Catalan friend shrugs. "His ship got back yesterday, like yours, so he can't have taken off again yet. You know how exasperating Miquel the Stickler is about making his crews get a proper rest between trips."

The maglev car decelerates one last time, almost imperceptibly (inertial absorption blocks, ultrafine tuning of the Algolese gravitic controls), stops in front of the wide platform at the foot of the phallic tower of our Department of Contacts, and opens its sliding doors.

"Up we go," I say to Narcís as we walk in, and to calm our nerves I repeat the rusty old joke, "It takes the express elevator at least two minutes to reach the top—we'll get to experience all over again how a sperm feels when it's ejaculated."

Narcís answers the joke in the usual way: "So long as we don't shoot out through the central shaft, Cubanito. I didn't bring my parachute today."

"Hush. Come on, kid, take your mitts off me! I haven't forgiven you for that Evita business. Chill! I hear the boss. Knock it off, Josué!" Nerys is whispering all this into my ears in her sultry voice as she slips wetly from my grip and floats back to her spot on her antigrav platform, despite my efforts to hold her tight.

I'll never learn. For the millionth time my attempts to hold on to her succeed only in getting her clear mucus smeared all over my expensive suit. Good thing the gunk is odorless and dries quickly.

The things we do for mermaid love.

Sometimes I think I get pleasure from making her jealous. Even though she's got a tail and fins instead of legs (or rather, precisely because of this), the girl drives me crazy. I return to my own place, reluctantly.

As usual, the muttering and whispers suddenly die away in the hall filled with condomnauts (all of us annoyed by being urgently summoned here) the moment Miquel Llul, the feared and respected head of the Department of Contacts, walks in.

We really do respect him, though he was never one of us. Sex isn't his thing. As they joke behind his back, Miquel is so dry, he'd only be able to make Contact with a race of robots.

Still, I often wonder if he's descended from the great medieval Catalan sage Ramon Llull. The way this skinny fifty-something stoic has transformed the Department is nothing less than alchemy. In fact, turning lead into gold with the philosopher's stone is child's play next to converting a handful of the most undisciplined Contact Specialists in the Human Sphere into a highly disciplined team with genuine esprit de corps.

Well, for most of us, anyway.

I give a little side-eye to Jürgen Schmodt, who in accordance with our mutual unwritten pact has bitterly pretended I don't exist ever since I came here.

Esprit de corps, him? Not toward me, for sure.

Whether or not he's the great-times-nine-grandson of Ramon Llull, Miquel the Magnificent made himself crystal clear to us the last time the German and I tangled (so far) and almost came to blows, six months ago. Next time there was trouble, he warned us, we'd both be gone from the Department and out of Nu Barsa like a shot. No right of appeal, no chance for being let back in.

And we didn't think for one second that Miquel the Implacable would waste time keeping his word.

He doesn't give a damn if Herr Schmodt, born (make that cyborg-assembled) on the German planet of Neue Heimat, is one of only three fourth-gen condomnauts in the Department. Much less that I've made more First Contacts than almost any other Specialist under his command.

Jürgen wheels around as if he noticed me looking. Maybe he did—who knows what bizarre sensors his Neue Heimat designer-parents built into him. He fixes me with his icy stare (his eyes are gray today, not the blue he usually goes for), and displays all his teeth to me.

Is my worst rival smiling at me? I must be seeing things.

Or maybe he recently made Contact with one of the carnivorous, territorial Alien species that bare their teeth at each other as a threat, and he picked up the gesture from them.

But no: he really is smiling, with his arm almost lovingly draped over the shoulders of the well-tanned condomnaut dressed all in white who's standing next to him. I've never seen the kid before. Must be new. There's something oddly familiar about him, though. With his oversized Afro and his coppery complexion. Something vaguely Caribbean about him. Could be Dominican, Jamaican, Puerto Rican, or . . .

Miquel's authoritarian voice, amplified by the speaker system, cuts short my thoughts.

"Good morning, condomnauts. You know I don't like beating around the bush, so I'll be brief. This is no mere administrative meeting. You've all been called together to hear three pieces of intelligence." He pauses, and looming over the rest of the crowd, my friend Narcís gives me a conspiratorial wink. "One good, one bad—and a third that's just meh. The good news is something we've been waiting years to hear: an extragalactic Alien race has finally reached our Milky Way."

Wow, looks like Narcís was slightly off: this time he's not talking about possible evidence or dubious sightings; they really exist, and at last someone has . . .

"The bad news is, we weren't the ones who made First Contact with them. And when I say 'we,' I don't mean Nu Barsa alone. The whole human race," Miquel continues, honoring as always his reputation for implacability.

Shit, now we're screwed. If the Kigrans of Ophiuchus were first to make Contact with them, or those tightfisted Arctians, or even the paranoid Furasgans, it'll cost us all we have and all we'll ever have and more to get access, someday, to the damn intergalactic-range hyperengine. Well, there's always the consolation of knowing that those smug, arrogant Germans and Russians will also have to pay their weight in gold for it. Of course, they have whole planets at their disposal, so they've got a lot more resources to draw on than we poor Catalans do.

We poor Catalans. Hey, I like the sound of that. Almost believe it and everything.

"And the meh news is that the lucky ones were: the Qhigarians," Miquel concludes, unflappable.

A sigh of both relief and disappointment, if that's possible, goes up all over the hall.

It's not like anyone's surprised. Statistically speaking, there's no race more likely to make Contact with extragalactics than the tireless wanderers of the Milky Way.

Just as no one knows who the Taraplin Wise Creators were, likewise no one knows the home planet of their Unworthy Pupils. Also known as the Alien Drifters. You can thank our human knack with nicknaming for coming up with that one.

You run into their immense, rambling, peaceful, yet incomparably fast worldships—built of good, solid metal without a drop of force-field technology—in every corner of the Galaxy. There's loads of them, too. More than twenty thousand worldships have been counted so far. And there's millions upon millions of Qhigarians squeezed aboard each one of them. So many that few humans can stand to stay on a worldship for even a few minutes—that's how strong the stench of the crowd is.

No other Alien race has such an impressive fleet. The Qhigarians offer the size of their fleet (which incidentally demonstrates that they don't believe in birth control and aren't worried about overpopulation) as irrefutable proof that they never had a planet of origin and have always lived on their ships, from the day the mythical Taraplins took them under their wings, or created them—they never clarify this point.

Could be. They have no written records, but not even the annals of the oldest species in the Galactic Community, such as the Kigrans, contradict them.

Most exobiologists, for their part, are of the opinion that no sentient species could have come into existence already wandering through space, like Pallas Athena emerging fully grown and armed from the head of Zeus. This would support the general feeling that if the Qhigarians ever had a planet of origin, they left it so many millennia ago that they've forgotten where it was—or else they're keeping the secret to sell it to anyone interested enough in that piece of information to pay them what it's worth.

The episode in which Joaquim Molá managed to wrangle no fewer than twenty-five working hyperengines from them for just a trilingual dictionary and his cat could be considered an almost shameful exception in the trade history of the Unworthy Pupils. Even the wiliest traders in the Galactic Community consider the

Qhigarians particularly sharp negotiators, never giving anything away or even offering a good deal.

Except, of course, for the hyperengines made by their beloved Taraplins, so useful and at the same time so resistant to reverse engineering. The Qhigarians paradoxically seem to treat those engines with the same generous attitude some ancient Christian sects from Earth show for their sacred book, the Bible. They gladly contribute them, delighted to let everyone know about them and use them.

It's also very strange that the Qhigarians, despite their interest in trading all sorts of technologies, have never wanted to buy or sell, much less use, any sort of weaponry.

They are committed pacifists. Or cowards to the core, depending on how you look at it. They don't even have a hierarchical control structure so far as anyone knows. Considering how they're piled up inside their worldships, their democratic nonviolence probably helps keep them from getting caught up in horrific fights all the time over every little thing, the way members of almost any other species would do under similar circumstances.

Pacifist ethics aren't completely unique to them; at least a couple dozen other known races around the galaxy stubbornly advocate peaceful coexistence, even when threatened with annihilation. None have spread as far or become as important as the Alien Drifters, though. In an environment as competitive as interstellar trade, a species that refuses to resort to violence even under duress tends to be quickly relegated to the back row—that is, if they aren't rapidly, definitively, and irreversibly eradicated.

Did something of the sort happen to the legendary Taraplins?

Paradoxically, it is known that in the not too distant past (which on a Galactic Community scale usually means a couple million years ago or more), the Qhigarians held Alien slaves. Not just one enslaved Alien species, either, but several dozen races. They protest that it wasn't exactly like that; the slaves were merely clones, inspired by Alien DNA (or the equivalent, depending on the species), and they gave up this awkward practice as soon as they learned to control their own genome by following the teachings of (who else?) the Taraplin Wise Creators.

It could be pointed out, though, that they took their own sweet time—a few thousand years, that's all—in interpreting those teachings. So I don't put much faith in their story. Or is it that I find it hard to imagine how a nonviolent race could practice slavery?

In any case, it's a good thing Quim Molá gave them a dictionary and a cat, and not his DNA, for those first twenty-five engines!

And what luck we also have our Countdowns. I wouldn't like imagining a race of cloned *me*s surreptitiously created and enslaved by the Unworthy Pupils. Nobody'd better meddle with my DNA in particular, or human DNA in general.

But it isn't their thriving fleet, their antiquity, their trading prowess, their pacifism, or their commitment to living as galactic nomads that makes the Qhigarians unique as a species, but rather two other considerably stranger characteristics.

The first is that each and every one of their gigantic, densely populated, chaotic worldships—veritable hyperengine-powered archologies that can measure dozens of kilometers in length and shelter several million individuals—is essentially a world apart. Onboard temperature, internal design, air composition, humidity, and even gravity vary considerably from one ship to the next. I should know, having visited several of them.

Exobiologists hypothesize that their diversity is the accumulated result of millions upon millions of years of separate evolution. Whatever. The fact is, the Qhigarians on any given ship are unlike those on any other. Unlike in culture, unlike in language, quite unlike in anatomy.

Many condomnauts doubt that evolutionary isolation has much to do with this. Perhaps because the Alien Drifters sometimes adopt morphologies that look fairly . . . well, whimsical would be the nice way of putting it.

The anatomical differences between the crews of any two Qhigarian worldships can be greater than those between us humans and the Kigran leviathans. And any two of their languages can have less in common than Chinese and Catalan. This makes Contact with each of their worldships a real guessing game, basically like making another First Contact.

Of the roughly twenty thousand known worldships, we humans have had dealings with no more than six hundred or so.

Some Contact Specialists are convinced that the thing Qhigarians find the greatest pleasure in (apart from cheating their trading partners, I mean) is messing with the minds of condomnauts from other races when they make Contact.

The second unique characteristic of the Alien Drifters is closely related to the former. It's what makes them a species. In fact, if it weren't for this, nobody would ever consider creatures with such highly divergent morphologies to be members of a single race. Though some recent theories refuse to accept them as such, insisting that they must instead be a conglomeration or coalition of species with different origins linked by shared interests.

Which would automatically raise the number of known Alien species in the galaxy by several thousand.

The deal is that, despite their Babel of varied languages—which some linguists think are just a hobby, while others deny their existence or consider them a pointless joke—all Qhigarians are intraspecies telepaths, able to maintain telepathic contact with one another at all times, yet without coming to form a single mental entity. Nothing too unusual about that for an Alien race, to tell the truth: nearly a thousand species have been found to have this fantastic ability so far.

This, of course, is the reason they need no leaders. If all are one and one is all, what for?

It's curious, by the way, that while all pacifist species belong to their class of telepaths, it doesn't work both ways: the great majority of species endowed with telepathy are not pacifists. A fact that incidentally negates the ancient notions some human science fiction writers had in the twentieth century, that knowing what your enemy is thinking will prevent you from considering him your enemy.

Interspecies telepathy, for example, which allows for mental contact with members of other species, turns out to be much more exotic. Kigrans have it, as does the Evita Entity with which I just made Contact. We know of barely thirty members of the Galactic Community blessed with this extremely useful gift, which saves so much time and, more important, avoids the bothersome misunderstandings constantly generated by our translation software, which is good but not magic.

And, while we're on the subject: none of these species (well, we still don't know enough about Evita to be absolutely certain, but I wouldn't bet my life on the possibility) is what you might call exactly pacifist.

But while the telepathic abilities (intra- or interspecies) of *all* other races in the galaxy cease to function at a certain distance, usually no more than a couple of kilometers, the fact is that, through some mechanism that no human or Alien science has yet managed to explain, it seems that *all* Qhigarians on *all* the worldships in the galaxy, no matter how distinct their populations, no matter how far apart their worldships (and by far apart, I mean lightyears apart; the Milky Way is a massively huge galaxy) keep in *constant* mental contact with one another, in *real time*, thus forming a sort of single telepathic colonial supermind—and making an utter mockery of Einsteinian relativity.

They themselves explain it as an ability inherited from the Taraplins. Which is like not explaining anything.

An old condomnaut joke says that "ansible" may secretly be the Qhigarians' real name, or perhaps the name of their planet of origin.

If any two Qhigarian individuals could establish that sort of faster-than-light telepathic link between themselves, the other races in the Galactic Community probably would have forgotten all their scruples and gotten together many thousands of years ago to fall eagerly on the Alien Drifters, pacifists or not, Unworthy Pupils or not, even if their ships were the fastest in the universe.

A communication method that can erase relativistic distances just like that would be too valuable to allow a single species to monopolize it in such an egotistical fashion.

Fortunately for the Qhigarians, one of the few things that is well known about their telepathic colonial supermind is that the faster-than-light link only works when large populations are involved. That is probably why, exobiologist speculate, so many millions of them travel on each of their worldships. In order to maintain their unity as a race or supermind even at interstellar distances, they must need to have dense concentrations of individuals join their telepathic powers.

What's paradoxical and positive about this whole business is that if there's any Alien species that shouldn't be particularly interested in having a hyperjump engine capable of intergalactic leaps, it's the Qhigarians. Why would they want to travel beyond the Milky Way, at the risk of losing the integrity of their telepathic colonial supermind, if that is what already allows them to be, in a sense, present everywhere in this galaxy at the same time? Not to mention that, if they suddenly had to deal with competitors for Taraplin hyperjump technology, over which they hold a de facto monopoly, their business model could collapse. No matter how cheap they tried selling their inherited jump engines.

The thing is, they know that other races would bet their futures on contacting those extragalactics. So even if the Qhigarians don't have any personal interest in the information themselves, owning that information puts them in the perfect position to auction off the trajectory coordinates of the extragalactic visitors to the highest bidder.

Shrewd negotiators, the Qhigarians are compulsive traders. They seem to get extraordinary pleasure from buying or selling anything, even their own shadows. The Quim Molá affair was no isolated case: on more than a few occasions, human crews who have made Contact with their worldships with nothing new or valuable to offer them (aside from our precious DNA or our jealously guarded translation software, things that are simply *not* for trade) have ended up exchanging some useless trinket or doodad for another working Taraplin hyperengine.

Some condomnauts even suspect that the Qhigarian religion not only calls on them to honor and worship their vanished mentors, but also forbids them to let any group of other sentient creatures pass by one of their worldships without trying their hardest to trade with them.

So not all is lost yet. They're tough negotiators, but it's just a matter of combing the galaxy until we locate the first worldship full of Qhigarians, then immediately buying all the information about those extragalactic Aliens that they have (or wish to sell us). At whatever price they set. Which I'm afraid will be truly and terribly high.

After a brief pause to let us all reach these conclusions, Miquel Llul resumes speaking.

"The news of the Qhigarians' recent Contact with extragalactics was brought to us by the hyperjump cruiser *Salvador Dalí*. Unfortunately, in spite of the magnificent Contact that their Specialist made with the Alien Drifters, the three thousand tons of nickel-titanium thermal memory alloy in the ship's hold, which we gave them down to the last gram, wasn't enough to purchase their exact trajectory coordinates. The Alien condomnaut did hint, however, that we might be in for an unpleasant surprise when we found the aliens from beyond the Milky Way."

Wouldn't you know, those greedy Unworthy Pupils. If they were private detectives and you hired them to find somebody, they'd probably charge you separately for first and last names. An article made from nickel-titanium alloy recovers its original shape when it's heated, no matter how dinged up it gets. It's useful, valuable stuff. And three thousand tons! That's quite a fortune.

That hint about an "unpleasant surprise" smells too much like "don't bother yourselves, leave this to us" to be taken seriously.

Now, did Miquel say it was the *Salvador Dalí*? I've heard the name. I don't mean just the ship's namesake, the great twentieth-century surrealist. Let me wrack my brains . . . Of course: that's the latest, largest, best-armored cruiser in Nu Barsa's booming space fleet. And its condomnaut is . . . who else, Jürgen Schmodt. And here he is, still smirking at me with his blue eyes, full of what I now know is pure, contemptuous self-satisfaction. So he's the one who handled the "magnificent Contact" that Miquel mentioned.

Score a point for you, Kraut. But the race ain't over yet. Not by half.

"The Department of Contacts, under pressure from the Ministry of Space Trade and the full Govern of Nu Barsa, has therefore decided that, beginning immediately, as a matter of top urgency that shall take priority over any other previously assigned trade or exploratory mission, *all* available ships and *all* available condomnauts operating out of this enclave shall actively search for any Qhigarian ships out there. *All* Nu Barsa ships shall fill their holds with the most valuable minerals and manufactures in the habitat, to be used as bargaining chips in order to obtain from the Qhigarians the specific coordinates of the extragalactic Alien ship's trajectory through our Milky Way, and any other related data that may be of use, *at any price*. And, if possible, to carry out our First Contact with the extragalactics at once.

"That is all. All condomnauts: report to your respective ships as expeditiously as possible. Goodbye, and good luck."

The uproar that followed Miquel Llul's solemn declaration wouldn't have sounded out of place in the Roman Coliseum.

But Plain-Spoken Miquel refuses to answer any questions, turns his back on our protests, and ignores whatever curses are hurled his way. He leaves the restive hall with the same long strides as when he entered, and no one dares get in his way.

One reason my colleagues have started shouting and complaining is that, after long weeks on deep space missions, many (such as myself) were hoping for a little R&R in the tourism and recreation zones of the great orbital archology.

Another is the sheer thrill of the hunt. We've always known that some condomnauts are better than others: more imaginative, more capable at making Contact, more skilled at "sleeping together," better at negotiating, better at languages, more empathetic—or at any rate, luckier.

And whoever can manage now not only to get the trajectory coordinates for the extragalactic Aliens through skilled negotiations with the first Qhigarian worldship they find, but to make Contact with the visitors from beyond the Milky Way themselves . . .

Well, there's a street in Nu Barsa named after Joaquim Molá, but it's short, narrow, and very hard to find. The condomnaut who makes our First Intergalactic Contact, on the other hand, could seriously expect to have not only the greatest avenue in Nu Barsa, now known simply as the Grand Diagonal, named in their honor, but a whole section of moving walkways as well. (How does "Josué Valdés Avenue" or "Rambla Josué Valdés" sound?) Or even an entire city district.

Maybe they'll even put their name on the first habitable planet discovered in another galaxy that Catalan ships find. Why not?

"It isn't fair, Josué!" Nerys growls into my ear after slipping gracefully up to me on her antigrav platform. Thankfully she seems to have forgotten how upset she'd been about the Evita

Entity, because if there's anything I dislike in a woman, it's retrospective regret. "I just got back from my mission two days ago! I'd been gone for three weeks! Like I'm going to want to go right back out and start traipsing around space looking for a bunch of Aliens from some other galaxy!"

I give her a hug to console her (and to squeeze her a little while I'm at it, mucus or no, now that things are better between us). And then I hear a voice with a certain unmistakable accent.

"*Nein* obligation to respect order of Llul, *meine Fräulein.*" Just as I feared. Gloating over his minor partial victory, Herr Schmodt can't resist the temptation to twist the knife. "Also no point there is. *Ich* find Qhigarians, then Extragalaktischen find *ich, und* then . . . "

"And then you'd better find a Catalan dictionary, or Spanish at least, and learn how to fucking speak a little, ass. You're an insult to Cervantes and Marsé!" This from my friend Narcís Puigcorbé, butting in from behind my back.

Wow, did that ever hit the German where it hurt. His nanobot-ridden body might be the perfect instrument of his steely will, but the truth is that his brain still hasn't found its way around the Spanish language, much less Catalan.

But like they say, people in glass houses shouldn't throw stones. I really ought to take up Catalan classes again—it wouldn't surprise me if my near-total ignorance of the language of Juan Marsé (whom I've only read in Spanish, though to be fair he won the Cervantes Prize for Spanish literature in the early 2000s) is one reason why they still haven't given me my citizenship.

And while I'm at it, I could also get myself a red-and-blue Barsa t-shirt and pretend I haven't always hated soccer in every form. And learn to dance the *pasodoble*, or even better, the *sardana*! And let myself be seen in public eating *fuet* all year round, and *coca catalana* at Christmas, and generally make myself over as the perfect Catalanized immigrant brown-noser.

Oh, forget it. I made up my mind from the beginning that I'd either gain citizenship on the basis of professional merit or else take my talents to another enclave. This old Cuban don't speak no Catalan, never have and never will, okay? I may be an opportunist, but everybody has their limits.

Right now, a very upset Jürgen is muttering something unintelligible, in the language of Goethe would be my guess, and turning about-face to confront the kibitzer. Apparently he didn't recognize Narcís's voice and doesn't have the slightest idea who said it.

Because, as soon as he sees—his mouth slams shut.

Today Schmodt has gone for the typical Aryan look: blond, blue-eyed, and a muscular six foot three. Even so he has to look up to face the gigantic Puigcorbé, at nearly seven foot four and just under a third of a ton in body weight.

Suck on that, fucking nanoborg. How does it feel to be the short one?

I imagine that with enough metamorphosis and a significant expenditure of energy, the Teuton's sophisticated nanocomponents would let him grow taller than my friend—but obviously he'd be even thinner then. The bodily transformations his nanotech produces in him look miraculous, but they can't violate the law of the conservation of mass or create extra kilos out of thin air.

Narcís gazes down upon him with his characteristically beatific smile. Though the smile on his shaven round head, atop his colossal bulk, doesn't look quite so beatific now.

Nerys gives my arm a hard squeeze with her damp webbed hand. The tension was so thick, I could have made bricks if I'd had a mold. The mysterious young mestizo in the Afro and the white outfit who'd been standing with Jürgen earlier has also come over, evidently to back up his German buddy if any blows happen to be thrown—and now he looks me in the eye with an expression that can only be hate. A two-on-two fight? I'm sure we'll win it hands-down. Poor consolation if it means being forced out of Nu Barsa, even if the German gets kicked out, too. So I'm not going to start anything. I'll wait for him to take the initiative. That way, at least I'll be able to plead self-defense.

But the minute passes—and nothing happens.

"Haha, only because Miquel say expel," Jürgen growls in his horrid Teutonic Spanish, and he grudgingly leaves Nerys and me, proving that even he is capable of thinking about the possible consequences of his actions.

As for his sidekick, it takes him a few more seconds to drop the belligerent attitude. Meanwhile, he hisses at me in a hoarse undertone, "Today you got off. But we'll see you again soon, Zero."

¡Ay, por Shangó y la Virgen de Montserrat!

Now I know where I remember him from. Cuba. CH. Rubble City.

How did I miss it—those eyes, that obsession with white clothes and cleanliness. I thought he'd be dead by now, but no. I can't even imagine how, but he and his hatred have followed me to Nu Barsa and now, I guess, he wants to "avenge" his fallen idol.

It's Yamil's little brother. Yotuel Fullmouth Valdés.

Life sure is full of little surprises. So now he's a Contact Specialist, too?

Not only that, but the asshole has sided with none other than my worst enemy, Jürgen Schmodt.

"Devils of a feather flock together," Diosdado used to say back in Rubble City.

Does he show his appreciation for Jürgen's mentoring with the oral skills that made him so popular among the old pederasts on the highway near Rubble City? Wouldn't surprise me.

I think of Taraplins and Qhigarians. "Wise Creator" and "Unworthy Pupil." What a coincidence.

"Don't worry, he won't be bothering you for now. Neither will his hound," Narcís interrupts, resting his immense hand on my shoulder. "At least for now. That Nazi might not give a damn what happens to you, but he knows better than to ignore a command from Miquel the Implacable. And if you're the first to make Contact with the extragalactics, you'll be practically a god here in Nu Barsa. If that happens, who cares if he's one of the few fourth-generation condomnauts we've got? They won't let him so much as touch you with a rose petal."

"Then I'll just have to make Contact with them first, come what may," I muse out loud, absentmindedly caressing Nerys's dorsal fins, which are standing deliciously on end after the adrenaline rush from our confrontation. It has also left an odd, bitter, metallic taste in my mouth. "Even if I'm just a plain old first-gen plebe of a condomnaut. And an immigrant, to top it all off."

We all laugh together, blowing off the stress with guffaws.

This first-, second-, third-, fourth-generation stuff isn't just an obsession with numbering everything, and it's also not about who your parents and grandparents were.

Quim Molá, Narcís, and I are all first-gen Specialists, setting aside how much more famous our precursor is. Our bodies weren't modified to facilitate making Contact with other species.

Not even the layer of adipose tissue that Narcís has cultivated through his sedentary lifestyle can be considered an irreversible phenotypic alteration. Through diet, exercise, and a gastric bypass, it's possible . . .

Well, only just possible is all. I'm not sure even God or Orula could slim my friend down.

In the beginning, of course, all of us Contact Specialists were first-gen. But the same thing happened as with bodybuilding before steroids: it was too clean to last.

My slippery Nerys is a perfect example of the second generation. She was born 100 percent human, in the polluted ruins of old Barcelona, on Earth. But from her earliest childhood she was such a freak for aquarium fish in particular and aquatic creatures in general, her parents thought they might have a future condomnaut on their hands. So, filled with hope, they spent what little savings they had to send her to the Feather, Hide, and Scale Academy on the New Madrid orbital habitat, where the Catalans have signed mutual agreements to more or less make up for the lack of any Contact Specialist schools on Nu Barsa.

I hope Nerys has been better about keeping in touch with the people who sacrificed for her than I've been, for their sakes.

The girl was a real eye-opener: she got highest marks on the empathy and trade diplomacy exams, and even her exobiology professors admitted that she understood the anatomies and physiologies of many Alien species better than they did. No surprise, then, that she was the first Catalan to undergo body modification surgery (she volunteered for it). She emerged from it transformed, of her own free will, into the mermaid she is today: webbed hands, fins down her spine, tail instead of legs. When she's out of water she has to use an antigrav platform to get around. But her specialty was, of course, the many Alien species that evolved in aquatic habitats, which up to then had been a hard row to hoe for condomnauts. Her Alien partners generally hadn't been completely satisfied with "sleeping with" creatures so biotechnologically underdeveloped that they had to use cumbersome scuba gear and crude propulsion systems to survive and get around in their liquid environments. Oh, and best of all, she has her choice of breathing through lungs or gills. The newly minted Catalan mermaid quickly racked up an impressive record number of Contacts.

Nerys's surgery was so successful that over the next five years Nu Barsa and other enclaves saw a proliferation of all sorts of scaly lizard-men, furry bear-women, and other even stranger and more improbable hybrids who led the way in Contacts for years.

The only problem that kept cropping up was versatility. Nerys is unbeatable for making Contact in water, and even in zero gravity she doesn't do bad; but with Aliens from dry worlds, she's a total disaster, even with her antigrav platform. That just isn't her thing.

And it goes without saying that making Contact with methane-breathing species or energy-based life forms remains out of reach for her generation of condomnauts. There's a limit to how far surgery can take you.

As a result, since not even a large hyperjump cruiser can afford to carry a full staff of Contact Specialists ready for every possible combination of Alien life forms they might run into on their journeys, somebody thought of going still further.

The third generation was a daring leap: sidestepping the phenotype modifications and daring to go straight at the human genotype itself.

But transgenic chimeras were a huge disappointment. Bird-men, fluorine-men, and other such exotic creatures were so anatomically and physiologically distinct from your average Homo sapiens that they simply didn't *feel* they were human. Nor did they see why they should sacrifice themselves for humans. Besides, they lacked the rough-and-tumble versatility of first-gen Contact Specialists, whether academy-trained specialists like Narcís or plebes like me.

A few stubborn governments nevertheless persisted in this direction. But when a group of almost fifty South African bat–human hybrids hijacked a hyperjump cruiser from the astroport on Krugerland and disappeared, direction unknown, after expressing their desire to freely settle their own world far from all humans, it became as clear as glass that the third generation was a dead-end.

I hope those bat-humans are all thriving, wherever they may be. They were very brave—and very sincere.

But there was a growing need for new and better Contact Specialists. Humanity was constantly losing too many trading opportunities because our Specialists were unable to make Contact with more than a couple thousand races, of the tens of thousands that make up the Galactic Community. It was still beyond our reach to "sleep" with chloride breathers, inhabitants of high gravity worlds, beings composed of plasma, and other life forms that are relatively distant from human physiology. At least, without special technology.

But necessity is the mother of invention, so in 2187, Japanese and German biotech and nanotech teams, working independently of each other on the rich colonial worlds of Amaterasu and Neue Heimat, almost simultaneously created the first fourth-generation condomnauts.

These were cyborgs. Half human, half machine. But a conceptually new variety: it wasn't a matter of adding cybernetic limbs or computational systems, but of total integration. Each and every cell of these amazing individuals had been modified when their developing embryos were at the morula stage, by inserting a set of nanomachines that could drastically alter them. On receiving the correct encoded command, that is.

As the cells divide and grow in number, so do the nanomachines inside them, always maintaining a one-to-one ratio so that at maturity they retain their ability to metamorphose.

Jürgen Schmodt, the other 999 little Germans in Neue Heimat, and the 1,500 little Japanese in Amaterasu all grew up like regular children, with mothers, fathers, brothers, and sisters, feeling perfectly human. Well, perhaps with the addition of subtle but constant indoctrination to make them want to become condomnauts when they grew up, and with particular attention being paid to their grasp of human biology.

Then, at the age of fifteen, after they had taken batteries of tests that caused more than half the teenagers to drop out (their identity still remains a closely guarded secret), those who were judged sufficiently stable and ready to proceed were told about their dual nature as humans and nanocybernetic complexes.

They were also told about the urgent need for more and better Contact Specialists, about the noble goal of working as sexual ambassadors for their cultures. And then they were given the codes to control their own metamorphosis.

Again, more than half declined the honor—or found themselves unable to deal with their recently revealed, sensational powers. The former flatly refused to do it; the latter either died from some dreadful, uncontrolled metamorphosis or went crazy. Or in many cases, both.

But Jürgen Schmodt, another fifty-six Germans, and 113 Japanese made the conscious decision to become Contact Specialists, got over the trauma, learned to control their bodies at the organ, tissue, and cellular level, and are now the last word in the Contact business: "protean condomnauts," the fourth generation.

There's a good reason why they've been termed protean. So long as they have enough energy available (which is why they've each had biobatteries surgically implanted in them), Jürgen and company can drastically transform their morphologies and physiologies in a matter of minutes, from their resting, more-or-less ordinary human form, into a being with a fluorine-based metabolism, or into a form that has no problem moving under gravity two hundred times that on Earth.

Now, they still can't turn into beings of pure energy or of antimatter; but, man, it's still a remarkable step forward! The new Contact Specialists quickly proved their exceptional worth, catapulting Neue Heimat and Amaterasu into the indisputable scientific and technological leadership of humanity thanks to the patents they obtained through their sensational Contacts with both new and old Alien species.

Recalling the lessons of the Five Minute War, before the chasm between them and the other human factions grew so wide that their rivals might choose to unite and obliterate them in order to erase their advantage, the prudent and astute Germans and Japanese "generously" offered to rent out the services of their new Contact geniuses to other nationalities.

At a high price, of course. Jürgen Schmodt costs the Govern of Nu Barsa almost as much as all the other personnel in the Department of Contacts put together. And since the bastard knows it, and probably even picks up on our envy and how we glare at him with hatred when his back is turned, he never misses a chance to show us that he's worth every last credit of the fortune he earns.

In the year and a half he's been here, he's already made nine successful First Contacts.

A real record, isn't it?

But in my opinion, you need to have more than a body that you can reshape at will to be a good condomnaut. No, Contact is much more than that. It's like hypernavigation: more an art than either a sport or an exact science. And this obnoxious nanoborg, who's used to always winning, just doesn't have the sensibility to understand what art is.

Still, it was him, not me, who discovered that extragalactics have arrived in the Milky Way. . . .

"Josué, watch it with that neo-Nazi son of a transistor," Narcís warns me, serious, watching him walk away with his protégé, my old enemy Yotuel. "And his little friend, too. You've met that kid before, haven't you?"

Puigcorbé surprises me: under all that fat, he has an extremely refined sense of empathy.

"Yeah. It's an old story, from back in CH. I thought he had died," I answer reluctantly. Narcís is the closest friend I have, but there are things you don't share even with your best friend.

Then, in a desperate attempt to raise our spirits, I make a proposal. "Hey, everybody! Since we're going to have to sail tomorrow and comb the cosmos for who knows how long, what do you say we take our leave tonight the right way? How about a five-star dinner at one of those classy little restaurants on a lake somewhere? They say Maremagnum Nuovo has good fish now. Even octopus. And good Earth wine, too, so we can toast to our good luck on the hunt!"

"Bravo!" Narcís's bottomless stomach is always ready for the next feast. Especially if there's good Earth wine to wash it down. "Maybe you're a self-taught plebe, but your list of successful First Contacts is still longer than Jürgen's," he reminds me, laying an arm as thick as my thigh across my shoulders.

This, of course, raises my spirits a little.

But not as much as Nerys does when, stepping into the elevators we take down to the habitat's ground level, she whispers affectionately into my ear, "It doesn't matter who makes Contact with those extragalactics, Josué! I love you, and not that robotic German. And tonight I'm going to show you again how much. At your place! We'll use up your annual water allotment in the best way you can imagine!"

I'm smiling like the drog that subsumed the bisork, like the verastis that parasitized the kindo—or, sticking to clichés, like the cat that swallowed the canary (though I've never seen a canary . . .)—while I picture what awaits me.

I'll report to the *Gaudí* tomorrow totally exhausted. But the pleasure will have been worth every last ATP molecule I expend. Oh, to have a biobattery implant, like the fourth-gen proteans.

Pleasure, pleasure, pleasure. Wet, splashing pleasure. Nothing like sex with a mermaid. Especially if you do it in the bath, or best of all in the shower. Because in bed, with all the mucus they give off . . . Afterward, I've often had to throw out the sheets, and sometimes even the mattress.

"I smell another wild goose chase. The hypergraph doesn't pick up any jumps in or out for the past thirty-six hours. But there might be a very small worldship, or maybe one that's been here for longer than that," Amaya tells us, her voice sounding tired. "Let's check the gravimeter. No; just as I suspected, this is a clean, boring system, nearly deserted. Apart from the primary, it only contains a super-Jupiter with . . . "

Amaya, a statuesque, dark-eyed brunette, is strangely attractive despite her insistence on wearing her dark hair so short. If only she were a man, if only she had any interest in men. I wouldn't mind sharing a bed with a him like her some night.

" . . . with twenty-one satellites and—what's this?" Our Amaya's voice is suddenly tinged with interest, and half the crew, clustered behind her in the narrow instrument chamber, tremble with excitement. "Oh, right. Comets. Lots of them. How intriguing. Astrophysically speaking, I mean."

Nuria, the ship's astrophysicist, with blue eyes, chestnut hair, and skin so tan she might have been born in the Caribbean, squeezes her lips tight at this dig. (She was Amaya's partner until last year, and there's still some bitterness between them about the breakup, which wasn't altogether friendly.) But she remains stoically silent, stroking Antares, who purrs in her arms, blissfully oblivious to the tensions among us.

Our umpteenth disappointment translates into a chorus of sighs. Amaya's tone returns to its former monotone. "Nothing on the gammatelescope. Besides the emissions from the primary, I mean. Beta Hydri I think this would be, according to the old Earth star charts. Has anyone recorded its data on the ship's log? I can't do everything myself. Nothing in the x-ray range, either. Well, it's a blue giant, so that would be strange, wouldn't it? The spectrographs say that its one big planet has a totally boring hydrogen-helium atmosphere, with a liquid core of . . . "

"Drop it, Amaya," Captain Berenguer orders her with a yawn. "Who cares about the atmosphere of one more gas giant? Disconnect. We're outta here." He turns to the navigator. "Gisela."

"All ready for the next leap, Captain!" The freckle-faced, slender redhead jumps up enthusiastically. All she needs to do to complete the picture is stand at attention and salute, like they do in the Navy she served in until less than a year ago. "I haven't stowed the antennae yet, so we can execute a jump right now."

Not pretty, for sure, but she's got something. Oh, if only she were a man . . .

Well, if she were, I probably would have slept with her by now and wouldn't be wasting so much time thinking about it. Weird, huh?

Not the best time to be thinking about it, either: as usual, I'm getting lost in digressions and more digressions, at the exact moment when I should be focusing my attention.

A bit past the exact moment, in fact.

"It was reckless of you to leave the antennae out. A single micrometeor impact could have . . . " Amaya begins to scold. And we know she's right, but we also know that if Gisela had given in to Amaya's sexual advances a few months ago, instead of to our stuck-up sensor tech Jordi's, there wouldn't have been any complaints.

A delicate thing, group dynamics on a ship.

Captain Berenguer plays the conciliator, as always.

"Bah, it doesn't hurt them to stay out for a couple minutes. Nothing will happen, Amaya. You yourself said this system is clean. And leaving them deployed saves us time. This'll be our fourteenth lightning jump today; after the next one, we'll recharge the batteries." His tone shifts from friendly to authoritarian: "Stations, everyone! Hustle! Hyperjumping in one minute, starting . . . ." He glances at the chronometer, almost lost in the bustling instrument panel that is Amaya's undisputed domain, and at last he says, "Starting now! Destination, Gamma Hydri. We'll keep combing this constellation. Five seconds before the jump, we disconnect the artificial gravity! On your toes! That means you, too, Josué!"

Lots of things have changed on merchant ships since the times when they were propelled by oars or sails, but some stuff endures even in this era of hyperengines. Pushing, jostling, a call to action stations, Antares meowing in protest at being tossed like a ball from Nuria's hands to those of Jordi, his official owner.

We all rush to our places, the soles of our shoes slapping the corridor floors. There are ten of us on board the eighteen-thousand-ton *Antoni Gaudí*: hypernavigator, sensor tech, life support tech, conventional engine tech, captain, first mate, third officer, trade economist, astrophysicist, and me.

Most know at least two professions inside and out. For example, Amaya is not only the best sensor technician I've ever worked with, and a better than adequate planetologist, she's also the onboard medic. Of course, that doesn't mean what it did centuries ago; she just has a slightly better knack with automated medical care than the rest of us.

Jordi Barceló, our brawny third officer, Gisela's current partner and my secret nemesis, was in the Navy, so he's familiar enough with military tactics to serve as our gunner or infantry operative under the command of Rómulo, the first mate and weapons expert.

Manuel (Manu for short), our conventional engines specialist, is our golden-fingered handyman, able to fix almost anything, from a disintegrator to a toaster.

Nuria, the blue-eyed astrophysicist and Amaya's former lover, is also our computer programmer, though Captain Berenguer himself could do a respectable job of it if he had to.

I'm the only one with just one job. Condomnaut, and that's it. No other technoscientific skills worth mentioning. So when there's no Aliens around to make Contact with, and no need for unskilled assistance (like holding a hydraulic wrench while someone changes the gyroscope on an inertial engine), I can kick back and relax. Like now.

It's surprising how long a minute can stretch and how many things you can do in fifty seconds if you know every inch of the confined space on your ship. Just twenty seconds and I'm sitting in my armchair, safety mesh in place, pleasantly surrounded by the greenery of the ample onboard greenhouse-garden-gym. At forty-five seconds I'm joined by Rosalía, the trade economist and the second exobiologist on board (the first is Pau, our life-support tech, of course). A big blond, built square like a football linebacker, but very feminine—from what Jordi told me one night.

I really have to work on my bisexuality. Or homosexuality. Lately I've really been noticing women. More than men, in fact. Sweet Jordi, forgive me. I promise to be better. If you give me lots of kisses.

Come to think of it, could it be that I'm getting over my Karla-Rita complex? Or maybe I'm just turning into a hopeless gossip.

"Josué, *por Deu*! I don't know . . . how you can . . . stay so calm," she gasps, still panting from the run, while fastening her seat's safety mesh. "Did you catch the poison dig Amaya made at Gisela? And at Nuria, before? What an unbearable butch."

"We're all on edge, what with one random jump after another coming up dry," I try to excuse her. Keeping the peace. As an enemy, Amaya Serrat would be worse than Jordi Barceló.

"If we don't find something soon, the gravitic batteries won't be the only things that need recharging." Rosalía loves playing the alarmist, though when push comes to shove you can count on her calmness and professionalism. Besides, she's got a nose for good trade deals.

An unmistakable laxness in my body tells me the artificial gravity's turned off, and mentally I count down: nine, eight . . .

"Locating the Qhigarians or the extragalactics isn't my problem," I reply, trying to sound even-keeled, though jumps through hyperspace always get on my nerves a little. "When we find them, though, you'll all get to rest easy while I'm out there sweating buckets."

. . . four, three . . .

"Or out there pleasuring yourself." The understudy exo-biologist winks at me, perhaps remembering my recent encounter with the Evita Entity. And to think that for months I thought she was playing on Amaya's team. I like her, but one time on night duty I had to reject her with all the diplomacy I could muster. I didn't want to offend her, but two platonic relationships on one ship were more than I could handle. This bisexualism business has really complicated things for crews. Especially for me. Nobody has more complex complexes than I do. At least, that's what it feels like, which amounts to the same thing. "Besides, what makes you think we can just sit around calmly waiting while you make Contact? Too much depends on your sexual and diplomatic abilities, condomnaut Josué Valdés."

. . . one, zero!

Sometime back, in Rubble City, I read a description of hyperjumping in an old science fiction novel I'd gotten hold of. The guy who wrote it, Asinov or something, said that it felt funny, like suddenly being turned inside out.

Not bad, coming from someone born in an era when they'd only gone as far as the moon, using antediluvian chemical combustion engines.

Years ago, when my physicist "friend with benefits" Jaume Verdaguer tried to explain the hyperjump process, about which we actually know so little, he used a slightly different metaphor; he told me that the jump through hyperspace was like falling into yourself while doing a somersault. Clear as mud, right?

The point is, every time I've had to go through it—and in my eight years as a Contact Specialist, I've done it thousands of times—that's exactly how it's felt: like my skin was trying to trade place with my guts, then suddenly jumping back into place, leaving everything still throbbing.

It isn't much fun, for all that hardened old space dogs brag about finding it invigorating, and especially stubborn ones even speculate that it rejuvenates their cells. But in the end, it's a small price to pay for a form of travel that can almost instantaneously transport ships with tonnages in the tens of thousands for distances of hundreds of lightyears, you know.

Over the past three weeks, though, I've started to think that I've simply gone through too much "falling into myself."

"Pau, Manu, and Rosalía—you're on bridge duty until our next jump. General maintenance and recharging the gravitic batteries. The rest of the crew can visit the sensor chamber if you don't have anything more urgent to do." It's Captain Berenguer's voice, sounding tired.

"This better not be the time we get lucky or I'll miss it," the trade economist complains, mischievously slapping me on the butt as we split up and head down different corridors.

Some women just don't understand that a man can tell them *no*.

It's our twenty-sixth day on an exhaustive search of the sector assigned to us by the great Miquel Llul, Radiants 2034 and 2035, and still coming up empty. More than four hundred jumps through hyperspace, hundreds of lightyears traveled, and zilch. Nada. The Qhigarian worldships that usually swarm almost every quadrant you go in the galaxy are conspicuously absent. Weird.

And judging by the three radio beacons we've picked up when we've approached the neighboring sectors, the other vehicles in the Nu Barsa exploratory fleet are having as much luck as we are in the rest of the galaxy.

There are currently 1,053 ships with hyperengines registered in the Catalan orbital habitat's astroport, between corvettes, frigates, and cruisers. More than a thousand of them are engaged in this veritable Qhigarian hunt, with the aim of catching an extragalactic next. This is what I call an all-out effort.

It's a little scary to calculate the volume of trade this flurry of exploration has cost us. If we don't find those extragalactics soon, the other human enclaves are going to start suspecting what we're up to. Then Aliens, and if everybody gets in on it . . .

We're running a big risk. If anybody but us finds those extragalactics, the Nu Barsa economy could go into a tailspin before the end of the year.

But if, on the other hand, one of our ships gets to them first, we could be the first living beings in the galaxy to travel beyond the Milky Way.

One of our ships? What am I saying. It's *got* to be the *Gaudí* that finds them, and me who makes First Contact. That way I'll earn Catalan citizenship once and for all, get married to Nerys, and crush the hopes of that bastard Jürgen Nanobot and his little pet, Bitter Yotuel.

"There's 18,250 hyperjumps into the system, and not a single one out!" Amaya's astonished voice greets me when I walk into the sensor chamber, where I also find Captain Berenguer, Nuria, Gisela, Rómulo, and Jordi petting Antares—as ginger, lazy, pampered, and busy purring as ever, in spite of the excitement in the air.

"Who's throwing the party?" the Captain thinks out loud, then asks, "How many planets?"

"None, according to the catalog," Nuria is quick to answer.

"I'm going to look that up for confirmation," Amaya adds distrustfully as she diligently consults first her computer, then her pandemonium of instruments. "But, Captain, I find it suspicious to see so many hyperjumps in. Our last leap may have thrown the sensors off. I'd better check the hypergraph. It's more sensitive."

"Save it," Nuria insists, checking a couple of data points over her former lover's shoulder and pointing them out with retaliatory smugness. "The catalog isn't wrong. Gamma Hydri is a triple star; the gravitational tides must be complex and constant; there was never any chance for a protoplanetary nebula to form in this system. Your instruments are working properly."

"But not a single ship shows up in the telescopes or on the gravimeter," Amaya protests weakly. "Could it be . . . ?" And after a couple of quick manipulations, she triumphantly announces, "It turns out the catalog sometimes does make mistakes after all. There *is* a planet. And it's a big one. It's a solitary, at one of the system's Lagrange points. I'm running a spectrograph analysis on it now . . . Wow, this is strange. It's nearly the diameter of our Jupiter, but it's more than 90 percent metal! A real treasure. Too bad we won't have time to stake a claim on it."

"True—but there shouldn't be a planet there at all," Captain Berenguer points out in turn, intrigued. "Nuria's right: it's almost impossible for a planet to develop spontaneously in a triple system."

"It could be a rogue planet," Jordi speculates thoughtfully, still stroking his ginger tabby. "There aren't many of them in this zone, but if the star only captured it recently, it wouldn't show up in the catalog."

"Captured? Nuh-uh. It would have been attracted straight into one of the three stars and burnt up in its corona. You know how slim the odds are that a wandering planet—and a metal one, too!—could fall exactly into one of the Lagrange points of a triple system? And then happily remain there, if it didn't have an active course-correction system?" Amaya furiously brushes off his idea, completely in agreement for one fleeting instant with her former lover, Nuria.

"Negligible," the captain declares, then adds, raising his voice, "Pau. Leave the battery recharging for later. Manu. Activate inertial thrusters. Amaya will send you the coordinates." Then, looking at us all, he concludes in a worried tone, "I suspect this isn't a planet, but a bunch of Qhigarian worldships. No other species has so many. Or so much metal. So I greatly fear they've already learned the secret of the intergalactic hyperengine. I think they're gathering here, planning to use what they learned to escape the galaxy. All of them, all at once. And if there are 20,410 known worldships on record, I'd say we got here just in time."

"Less than one kilometer to docking. Approach is normal," I transmit after checking the telemeter on my space suit. I float without activating the jets; the minimal gravity intrinsic to the giant conglomeration of thousands of Qhigarian worldships is enough to attract me slowly toward the open airlock, the coordinates of which were almost reluctantly given to us by the Unworthy Pupils only a few minutes ago. Made of some translucent material, it's practically invisible against the starry background. "Amaya, you copy?"

"Perfectly, there's no interference at all. You know they don't have to use radio waves and they don't trust field technology. That airlock must be completely transparent to electromagnetic waves," Amaya replies. She's my remote Contact operator today, praise Shangó. As a little hologram on my helmet visor, she smiles as if ready to instill all the confidence I need in me. "Josué, I really do wish you luck. You're a good guy. If only you were a woman . . . Well, nobody's perfect, right?"

"Then I'd be heterosexual." I parry her joke, sticking out my tongue. "We could have been the couple of the millennium, but as things stand, impossible."

"¡*Viva la tolerancia!* We'll talk it over in my cabin after you get back." Amaya keeps the joke going with a wink. "But for now, heads up, you're almost there."

On my final approach to the inlet hatch for the titanic Qhigarian complex, I break my momentum with a brief flaring of my initial engines and alight on the threshold of the lock.

One more tiny jump, which in this microgravity takes only a quick flex of my muscles, and I'm inside.

The hatch, made of the same translucent material as the rest of the airlock, seals quickly and silently behind my back as soon as I advance a few meters across the nearly invisible material, to which the magnetic soles of my boots nonetheless adhere perfectly well.

Wow. A metallic plastic? It's going to turn out these Qhigarians are also experts at polymers. Did they inherit that from their

Taraplin mentors, along with almost everything else? Or maybe they picked it up from trading with the Furasgans, who have a reputation for being good chemists.

The sensors in my suit tell me there's enough external pressure for me to take off my helmet. I do so. I don't take off my translation earphones, though. Qhigarians have an almost morbid curiosity in every language they run across, including our universal translation software. That's weird for a telepathic species, isn't it? Also weird that they have as many spoken languages as they do worldships.

Yes, there are plenty of odd things about these Unworthy Pupils of the Wise Creators.

As was to be expected, the air has the "previously used" smell typical of something that's been recycled a thousand times. It must have passed through the breathing sacs of billions of Qhigarians before it got to my lungs. But as if to make up for that, its oxygen content is slightly higher than that on Earth.

Once more it occurs to me that Quim Molá didn't have such a hard time of it on that mythical First Contact when he got the hyperengines. Almost humanoid, breathing nearly terrestrial air. Lucky Catalan devil.

I keep moving forward. One lone man, wearing an ultraprotect suit but holding his helmet under his arm, walking to make Contact through a small patch of atmosphere trapped between nearly invisible walls, beyond which stretches the vacuum of space. The daily grind, in other words.

To my left, the three stars of the Gamma Hydri system, intent on their endless ballroom dance. Ahead of me, the immense sphere made from the agglutination of thousands upon thousands of enormous Qhigarian worldships. They've got 20,034 here already, and more keep arriving every minute. If Captain Berenguer is right and they're just waiting until they're all together in one place before they take off, I'd better hurry.

This Contact will be admirably brief.

A vague shadow approaching from the other end of a long series of translucent partitions, which open as it reaches them and close as it passes through. Here comes my partner for the day.

Now I get the usual sweating, itching, and trembling. I was wondering when it would start.

What'll it be like? I've made Contact with Qhigarian worldships a dozen times in my career, and I've met with almost everything, from a worm with a huge composite eye and ten pairs of vestigial legs to blue humanoids with scales in continuous motion, and between them there was a sort of blind, fuzzy bear with just six limbs. There were two of the bears, now that I think of it . . .

The worst was the starfish-octopus with the slimy tentacles all covered with eyes. Hope I don't get that one today.

I can see it now. Purple, a little smaller than me, central body, multiple extremities branching out through bifurcation, covered with eyes, doesn't touch the ground. That would explain the microgravity. Shit.

My luck's run out. It *is* that thing. The most disgusting symbiosis you can imagine, a starfish joined to a slimy octopus, nearly six meters from tip to eye-encrusted tentacle tip.

"God damn fucking shit," I mumble, annoyed.

"What is it, some new form?" Amaya's holographic image, now projected directly in the air before my eyes, frowns with worry. "Calm down, Cubanito, your heart is racing. Listen, Josué, if the translation software doesn't recognize its language, I can always call on the full processing power of the ship's central computer to help you out."

It's good to feel like someone has your back at times like this, even at a distance.

"No," I sigh, resigned. "It won't be necessary. It's not a new morphology. Not new at all."

Nerys might have enjoyed it, I guess. After all, it looks like an aquatic form.

But as for me—yuck! We all have a right to our own preferences, don't we?

I remember Contact with the last little fucker like this as one of the most difficult, most disgusting I've ever experienced. Lacking any sexual orifices of its own, the damn "Unworthy Pupil" spent the whole time slowly coiling its myriad slimy, bifurcating ocular tentacles all over my body, and not just on the outside. Good thing its mucus serves as a lubricant, because otherwise I would have gotten hemorrhoids and esophagitis at a minimum. That's right, a Contact Specialist's job isn't always a pleasant one.

But the automatic translator clearly understands its language. At least that's something.

"Hello. Josué, human ship *Antoni Gaudí*, Nu Barsa. We wish to negotiate trajectory coordinates of extragalactics," I say, trying to be as concise as possible to make it easier on the translation software, which turns my words into a cacophonous series of squeaks and chirps, like a cricket making sweet love to a high-tension wire.

The tentacular creature gently moves its multiple eye-encrusted arms with a certain ethereal grace that sort of reminds me of a patch of seaweed stirred by a slight current.

And here comes the second storm of click-squeaks: "Valaurgh-Alesh-23, worldship Margall-Kwaleshu, Qhigarian. Barter-deal, offer, what?" The sentences come over my earphones in the usual twisted and mutilated syntax. This is the best the automatic translator can do: plain verbs, no prepositions, no conjunctions. And in an incongruent soprano pitch.

I'll have to remind Nuria, who programmed the translator, that dubbing a purple octopus with a porn star's voice doesn't sweeten the bitter draft of making Contact with it.

At least this isn't the same octostar as last time, or it might think I like playing this game.

"Deuterium 180 tons and tritium 120 tons," I toss back to Valaurgh-Alesh-23, in order to impress it with how much fusion fuel we are offering, and to maintain my advantage I immediately follow with, "Do we proceed?"

"Material no-proceed." The "no" sounds worse in this voice. "Deal no-interest."

Amaya makes no comment, but her clenched teeth and furrowed brow show more clearly than a thousand words that she wasn't expecting such a clean refusal, either.

Material no-proceed? Deal no-interest? What do these guys want, the philosopher's stone? Those three hundred tons of heavy hydrogen isotopes are practically all of Nu Barsa's reserves, enough fusion fuel to last any worldship a whole year. And this nasty . . . Valaurgh rejected it like I was offering a pile of sand.

Think quick. We can't let them leave the Milky Way without telling us where the extragalactics are. We could allow Rómulo and Jordi to test the strength of our weaponry against this peaceful cluster of worldships until they reveal the secret to us. That would amount to a sleazy protection racket trick, especially since they don't have any way to respond in kind, as everyone knows. But big problems call for big solutions.

And if they still refuse to negotiate and insist on leaving, then what? Wipe out twenty thousand worldships? With trillions of sentient beings on board? That would be genocide, and the entire Galactic Community would come after us.

No, violence is the last refuge of the incompetent. There's got to be something else they really want. Some offer they can't refuse, even if they're leaving the galaxy.

That's it. I know what can do it.

Should I consult Captain Berenguer? No time for that. Anyway, a Specialist is the only one capable of assessing a Contact. I'll risk it, then. Miquel said *at any price*, after all.

I swallow hard and present a new proposal, excited.

"Current human translator, with data of 11,568 Alien languages."

"*Qué cojons, tío?* What the fuck are you up to? You can't give them our software!" Amaya cries out, stunned. But a second later she calms down and I can almost see her shrugging, though the holocamera only captures her face. "All right, okay. It's an idiotic trade, but you're the condomnaut, you're the negotiator. If this helps us locate the extragalactics, it'll have been worth the price. Those Unworthy Pupils had better take it, for their sake. Otherwise we'll have to fire on them with everything we've got."

Damn, so it's not just me thinking that way! I feel slightly relieved to find I'm not the only potential genocidal maniac in the crew.

Now the asterocephelopoid freak is flailing about, almost hysterical with greed, telepathically hashing it out with its fellow creatures, I suppose (since Qhigarians, as colonial telepaths, don't have anything like leaders or bosses). Finally, after another concert of chirps and clicks and squeaks, it extends a tentacle toward me with a shower of sparks coming out at the end.

I got you, you ambitious thing. When I have unlimited funds to negotiate with . . .

I recognize what it's holding, of course. It's a universal computer compatibility device, made by the Arctians, that can read or transfer data between any two systems without connecting them by cables. Used throughout the galaxy to avoid computer incompatibility problems.

Everybody has a price, and it seems that an offer of 11,568 computer-coded languages is too tempting for Valaurgh-Alesh-23 and its people to keep pretending they're not interested.

It's an impressive total, but I wonder if they realize it includes about six hundred of their own dialects.

I imagine they do. And if not, well, caveat emptor, as the Romans used to say. Not telling the whole truth might look like lying, but it isn't quite the same thing. All's fair in love and trade.

Concealing my self-satisfaction, I let the enchanting Valaurgh caress my neck and twine its tentacle around my earpieces. I try to stay still, though the sparks from the Arctian device are tickling me, or maybe it's the sucker-eyes on the mucus-coated tentacle. I don't know and don't want to know.

"Translator assimilate here-now," a squawking voice surprises me. It seems to emerge from within the thicket of waving tentacles. What kind of vocal organ does this star-octopus have, that it can enunciate so clearly in addition to making clicks, chirps, and squeaking noises? "Two informations interest humans, negotiate-trade proceed. One: Qhigarians-all leave galaxy now-future, destiny-future no-negotiate. Two: Qhigarians no-here-future, hyperjump no-work here-future. Taraplin hyperengine no-true before-here-future. Taraplins no-true. Qhigarian mind teleporter, hyperengine yes-true."

Shit. I hope I got that wrong. It can't be . . .

"Holy *cojons*," Amaya mumbles, jaw on the floor, eyes popping out. It seems that, in spite of the messed-up semantics produced by the translation software, I understood correctly. "Josué, I need confirmation. First, they're all leaving, and there's no way they're going to tell us where to."

"Correct," I say in a thin, strangled whisper. "Captain Berenguer figured it out. He's good. They're going, and they don't want us to know where. They're playing it safe. Maybe they're scared of the extragalactics. Or of us."

"Scared of us? Why? And what was the second point? I don't think I quite got it." The sensor tech's normally self-assured contralto voice shakes, full of anxiety, and her left cheek has a slight tic. "The Taraplins never existed? Then how did they make those hyperengines?"

"They didn't make them," I snort. "The Taraplins didn't exist, never existed, and they have nothing to do with the black hole at the center of the Milky Way. The so-called hyperengines are just metal cans with self-destruct mechanisms, that's all. The Qhigarians, the Unworthy Pupils themselves—and I still don't see why they made up the whole story about the 'Wise Creators'— are the ones who created the fake hyperengines. It was them all along, making all our jumps through hyperspace possible with their minds. They're teleporters! The only ones in the Milky Way! Shit, Jaume Verdaguer and his crazy friends were right."

Amaya looks at me for a long time in silence, then finally dares ask, gently and almost in a whisper, as if she really wants to know, "Josué, who is Jaume Verdaguer?"

"Oh, God, Amaya, that doesn't matter now," I spit out, staring at smug, pompous Valaurgh-Alesh-23 with a growing temptation to tie it up into a giant knot with its own tentacles. I finally explain, "Old friend of mine. A physicist who never believed in the story of the Taraplins and their hyperengines."

"Oh," is all she says. Then, as the gravity of the situation dawns on her, she adds, as if still in doubt, "So there are no Taraplins, no hyperengines, just Qhigarian teleportation." Her voice is trembling more than before. "And as soon as the last one leaves, we'll be stuck here, unable . . . unable. . . ." She can't say it out loud.

"Unable to get home. Unable to travel faster than light," I tonelessly complete the thought she couldn't get herself to say. "Which practically means the end of the Human Sphere as we know it, and of the entire Galactic Community for that matter. Imagine! Poof, no more hyperjumps. Complete isolation between colonies, enclaves, and Earth. Same for every Alien race. Unless we manage to contact the extragalactics first, that is, and they have hyperengines that really work—and not mentally, if I had my choice. Assuming they want to sell them to us, naturally. That's a lot of 'ifs' to work with, don't you think? I'd say we're good and screwed."

"Fucking Qhigarians. We should blast them all out of the cosmos for conning the whole galaxy for so many millennia. They can't leave now, just like that!" Amaya growls in pure rage at finally confronting our brute reality. But she instantly calms down, moves off holocamera to consult something, then returns to inform me mechanically, "There are now 20,112 worldships in this system. They're still arriving." She tightens her lips with determination. Something about the Catalan ability to put a good face on a bad hand and rise to meet the toughest challenges fascinates me. No wonder they've come so far. "Josué, if the octopus is telling the truth, there's just

300 more to come. At the current rate, that gives us about . . . two hours. Listen up: if that sleazeball gives you the trajectory coordinates for the extragalactics in the next five minutes, we can still pull this off."

Now, that's what I call quick tactical thinking.

"We've got to do it," I agree. Then, turning to slimy, purple Valaurgh-Alesh (I hope the other twenty-two from its brood or whatever are all dead), who continues fluidly waving its weightless tentacles, I insist: "Essential to have trajectory coordinates for extragalactic ship, here-now."

The damn Qhigarian is so . . . Qhigarian, it waits a good three seconds before answering. And, it seems to me, it's managing better than before with its newly acquired translation software. "Information available. Translator, no-sufficient price. Offer, what more?"

Oh, fuck Shangó, Orula, and La Virgen del Pilar. Clever bug, it was just messing with me. It fed me the key piece of information, enjoyed watching our faces as we figured out how they'd been swindling the whole galaxy for millions of years; and now it refuses to tell me what I need to know. What do I do now?

It's like knowing you're about to die and knowing what medicine you need to save your life, but not where to buy it.

"Assholes! Tell them, if they don't let us know where those guys are right now, we're going to tell the whole Galactic Community about their con game, and we'll all get together and reduce them and every last ship of theirs to scrap!" Amaya explodes, her lovely dark eyes shooting fire.

"Chill out," I try to calm her. It's my turn to pretend to be cooler than I feel, while my neurons work feverishly. "Threatening them won't do any good. Don't you realize they literally have us by the balls? I wonder if any Alien species already suspected. They'll owe their own Jaume Verdaguers a huge apology. For me, I'm planning to get a statue of him built while he's still alive, if we get out of this."

"I'll help you," Amaya offers, obviously in need of something concrete she can do. "I've got a friend who's a sculptor."

"Look. There's nothing we can do to pressure them, and no threats that could work. Nobody can make a hyperjump without their help. So if we try to attack them, I wouldn't be surprised if they teleport us to the other side of the galaxy. Likewise, if we try to leave now and warn the others about their con game, they'll have no trouble stopping us. Anyway, as soon as they're gone, the whole Galactic Community will figure out for themselves what they were up to; we won't have to tell them. Except it'll be too late by then to do anything about it."

"And then what?" Amaya says impatiently, almost in tears from anger and frustration. "We give up, call off the search, forget about the rest of humanity, since losing our hyperengines is just about as fucked-over as we could possibly be, and stay for the rest of eternity in this system without any oxygen planets to colonize? The closest star to us from here is four lightyears away."

"No." I smile, in the sudden certainty that I've found the solution to our problem. "I'll pay them more for the information we want. 'Unworthy Pupils'—a perfect name for them! Even if their 'Wise Creators' never existed. What else do we have that might interest them?"

"Pay them more?" The sensor tech's eyebrows almost disappear into her short but luxuriant dark mane. "But they already rejected enough tritium and deuterium to fuel a ship for a whole year, and we just gave them our translation software. I don't see what else we have of value."

"DNA," I interrupt her, smiling mischievously. "The only other human possession that the Qhigarians have always been interested in obtaining." Turning to the Contact Specialist star-octopus, I carefully articulate, "Human DNA, trade for trajectory coordinate extragalactic ship."

The frenzy of activity running through Valaurgh-Alesh-23's thousands of slippery, bifurcated, eye-encrusted tentacles is more than enough proof that it is seriously analyzing the proposal—with the help of all the other minds on all the Qhigarian worldships. Determined to convince it, I point out, "New galaxy, conditions unknown. Qhigarians need new race slave-clones."

"Price sufficient," my tentacular interlocutor replies at last, sounding almost sad. "Extragalactics trajectory, coordinates, transmit here-now." And with that, it transmits a long string of numbers, which the computer in my suit and its big brother on board the *Gaudí* record flawlessly.

Then the Qhigarian adds, almost sarcastically, "Second transmission-coordinates extragalactics-trajectory."

Shangó and Oggún! So we're the second ones they told? The second to get a crack at finding those guys?

Time to run, then. With any other species, I'd dare ask who they gave the information to, Aliens or humans, and if humans, what enclave they're from and which ship. But the Unworthy Pupils would make us pay for each crumb of information. And unfortunately, we have no bargaining chips left.

It gave away the fact that we're not the first they told out of pure sadism, obviously.

"We did it!" Amaya laughs, excited, missing that last bit of bad news. I'm not planning to dampen her joy. Everybody will hear it when they replay the recording. "The computer is interpreting the coordinates and putting together a linear trajectory. What I can tell you now is that our visitors come from the Large Magellanic Cloud, they're seeking out yellow dwarf stars, and their hyperjump system is long-range and very precise. I'll have more to tell you later. For now, when you make Contact with that disgusting octopus, better hurry up and give it your DNA. I imagine that the fewer worldships there are remaining to join this conglomeration, the harder it will be for poor Gisela to find a feasible jump trajectory."

She's right, of course. Though damned if I want to go through the ordeal of getting myself coiled up in and screwed over by this snot-covered Qhigarian octopus-starfish with too many arms.

I almost feel like running away, like I did when I left Rubble City. Now that I've got the extragalactics' trajectory coordinates, I'll just refuse to make Contact and we'll hightail it out of here. It's what they deserve; not a bad idea to play one last trick on these tricksters.

But I have a sneaking suspicion that if we don't play fair, they'll just send us wherever they feel like and not where we want to go, giving the other searchers an even bigger edge on us than they already have. So I choose the straight and narrow. Sucks to have principles.

"Shall we proceed?" I finally suggest, sighing with resignation while I start to undo my suit. The faster I get through with this the better. Good thing it'll be quick and painless to collect epithelial cells with useful DNA by swabbing my oral mucous membrane. Making Contact with this Valaurgh is going to be unpleasant enough already.

"Extragalactic trajectory data, transmitted. Human DNA no-degraded, required," the Qhigarian calmly announces, without making the slightest effort at approaching me.

What? For a second I'm stunned, then I understand and laugh out loud.

Of course, human DNA no-degraded: I forgot about my Countdown.

Even if I turn off the handy device right now, its vibrations have already synchronized with my biofield, so my DNA will continue to degrade when it's away from my body, and therefore become useless to the Qhigarians, for the next hour at least. And it's not like we have time to spare.

"Human DNA no-degraded, required, cloning," the octopus repeats, relentless. "Do, give sample, here-now."

"What the fuck does the freak want now?" Amaya splutters. "Your DNA isn't good enough for it?"

Shit. I think I'm going to have to stay in this crappy little system a little longer.

"No, it's the Countdown I'm using," I sigh, and I turn off the ultrasound-emitting collar that hangs around my neck. "Oh, well. You guys go on. I'll wait here until the effect wears off and they can take a usable sample of my genome. An hour isn't so long. You can come back later."

And if we don't find them in time, nobody can say that Josué Valdés wasn't a team player.

"No way," Amaya says between gritted teeth. "You're the Contact Specialist. We're going to need you there when we find the extragalactics. Besides, not only do we not have an hour to waste, we might not even be able to make it back here and get you if these Unworthy Pupil con artists take off." She swallows hard, tries to smile confidently. "So—I'll stay. I hope they drug me up, because I don't like pain, and I can't stand the thought of being fingered by those thousands of arms covered in eyes."

You're a real hero, Amaya. What a sense of duty. Everything for Nu Barsa and Catalonia, no?

Touched, I'm about to thank her for the gesture, but then I get a better idea.

"That's the spirit, Amaya. But I don't think I can allow you to make such a sacrifice." I wink mischievously. "On any exploratory mission, especially one to make Contact with extragalactics, a sensor tech is also more useful than . . . than an arrogant third officer who anyway doesn't know how to do anything but fire his guns, don't you think?"

Yes, revenge is a dish best served cold. Amaya's eyes shine conspiratorially. She smiles and says, "I'll consult with the captain, of course, but I think your proposal will strike him as perfectly acceptable. I almost feel sorry for the Qhigarians, though. Cloning Jordi Barceló for slaves won't do them a lot of good, wherever it is they escape to."

It's cold.

Real cold.

I shiver, maybe because I'm naked as a worm, huddling by a pitiful little bonfire.

I once read that our senses of heat and cold, feel, and taste play only a small role in the architecture of dreams. But I also know this must be a dream. A frozen dream?

Still, I almost feel like rejoicing. Though my teeth are chattering and my scrotum feels like it's trying to hide inside my body, at least this isn't my classic, obligatory nightmare, with my colorless Atevi losing the mutant cockroach race to Yamil's long-legged Centella yet again and me being forced once more to copulate with the fat girl-Doberman Karla-Rita.

Maybe I'm finally going to get over it.

But it's so, so cold. Too cold.

The fire's going out, I'll have to feed it. Luckily, there's a little pile of logs here that look like they ought to burn well. If there's any logic to this dream at all.

If not, maybe they'll turn into snakes when I touch them, or into sand, or . . .

Nothing for it but to try. Let's see if things really have changed for the better in my REM department, or merely . . .

Here goes the first log . . . Good; it isn't trying to bite me or dissolving into foam. How strange! It calmly lets itself get tossed onto the fire, and when it lands in the flames . . .

Yeah, I was starting to wonder. Instead of burning like it should, it shudders, acquiring the features of my friend Abel. His black skin writhes, scorched by the tongues of flame, and he asks me, "Why'd you do it, Josué? Why'd you abandon me?"

Shit, now I know where this new nightmare is heading. Pure remorse. Everyone on the bonfire, sacrificed for one thing only: me and my well-being. Step on up, ladies and gentlemen, watch everyone else burn so that Josué Valdés, the Rubble City Egomaniac, can live and prosper.

But I still can't stop. No point getting scruples now. Especially since it keeps getting colder and colder. All I can do is throw another log on the fire. And another, and another.

Every time the bark of a log touches the fire it convulses and turns into the face of somebody I know. They cry out in pain as they burn, scolding me for being a cynical, ungrateful egotist. My childhood friends and enemies from the poorest neighborhood on the outskirts of CH: Yamil, Evita, Diosdado, Damián, Karlita . . .

And Agustí Palol, the likeable captain of the hyperjump corvette Juan de la Cierva; and the young physicist Jaume Verdaguer; and Nerys, the mermaid condomnaut; and Narcís Puigcorbé and his *wife Sonya; and Captain Ramón Berenguer; even Third Officer Jordi Barceló. All are consumed by the greedy flames until I have no one left to throw on the fire, nobody else to sacrifice to the gods so my heart can keep on beating and not freeze solid.*

But I still feel cold, and strangely the firewood hasn't run low. So I throw on another log, and another . . . And once more I hear screams, accusations; but now the voices are all mine, the faces dissolving in the voracious blaze all have my features, because I've sacrificed so much of the best part of me to get this far, so I'm the one burning, with a smell of scorched flesh that turns my stomach. It's burning, burning—I can't go on.

A reflux of bile burns my esophagus, but when I try to spit it out I can't stand up, I'm held too tight by the security net on my seat in the greenhouse-gym.

One second of suffering, just one, and the bile dissolves at some point between the pain and my mouth, but it doesn't turn into vomit; it makes my eyes water, but my insides settle into their regular resting places.

I still hurt, though. Top to bottom. The price of Contact with that horrid, slimy Qhigarian star-octopus. Good thing the automedic already fixed up the worst of it, but . . . Jordi wasn't the only one who made a sacrifice for Nu Barsa, Catalonia, and humanity.

Of course, I do hope that after the Unworthy Pupils take his DNA, they'll free him before leaving the Milky Way, hurting only his ego. And I hope he'll forgive us someday for leaving him behind. Me, Amaya, all of us.

And if not, screw him! He deserved it, the bastard.

So we're finally making the leap—and once more I realize how right people are to say you should always stay awake during a hyperjump. It seems that the hyperengine, or rather the Qhigarian hive mind, can do serious side damage to the sleeping psyche among sentient species.

Though it's not like I could help falling asleep after all that commotion, what with Gisela taking more than an hour to find a workable series of hyperjumps to get us where we wanted to go.

It really isn't her fault; with nearly 90 percent of these trouble-making Unworthy Pupils gathered at a single spot in the galaxy, it's incredibly difficult to make hyperspace leaps (or rather, teleportations). And they're harder to bear, too. Well, pretty soon we'll miss them, I bet. At least the Qhigarians were polite enough to transport us here, as a kind of farewell gift. Wherever here is . . .

Is this the last hyperjump? Could we already be at Lambda Trianguli?

I glance at the clock in the greenhouse. An hour and twenty-two minutes . . . It's been nearly two hours since we left the conglomeration of Qhigarian worldships, and we've only managed to complete three jumps. There were 20,181 ships when we left; I don't think we have much time to continue our search. Unless the Alien Drifters were just lying to us again about how hyperjumping really works.

Qhigarian assholes. Smart of them to take off. I almost feel like hunting them down all over the Metagalaxy, once we get the extragalactic hyperengine. And if we ever get our hands on them . . .

Even after hearing their confession myself, it's hard to believe they had everybody fooled for so many thousands of years. Why would they lie like that? Were they afraid of being enslaved if they admitted that their telepathic colonial supermind was the real hyperengine, and that the Taraplin Wise Creators never existed? Were they really all one species? Did they come from a planet like everyone else, and were they jealously guarding the secret? Or did they evolve on their ships, or perhaps come from another galaxy? If they're telepathic, why are they so obsessed with languages?

So many questions, and maybe we'll never learn any of the answers. Though I have a feeling that the paths of those Unworthy Pupils and humanity will cross again someday. The cosmos is big, but not infinite.

Or at least let me believe it isn't. The human mind can't handle infinity. At least, not mine, not now.

Right now, of course, we've got bigger fish to fry.

I run to the sensor room and arrive, panting, in time to hear Amaya say, " . . . Trianguli. Red dwarf, six planets, asteroid belt. The hypergraph shows only one ship entering—none leaving. No need to be exact; we're lucky the hypergraph still works at all," she reports, unfazed. "But there's also a strange energy signal"—now her voice shakes, as if she's afraid we've been fooled again. "I've never seen anything like it. I think . . ." We all tense up around her. "Let's have a look through the gammatelescope. Ah. Good news: there's an identity beacon from one of our own on the scanner. The entering ship is human."

"Shit," Captain Berenguer enunciates clearly. Always so polite.

So the other guys the Qhigarians sold the information to were human. And obviously they beat us here. Well, Aliens would have been worse. Is it the Germans? The Japanese?

"The ship is ours," Amaya confirms, greatly relieved, after checking the signal. "From Nu Barsa, I mean. The *Miquel Servet*."

Just my luck. Did it have to be the hyperjump cruiser that my Nerys serves on as condomnaut?

I look at Captain Berenguer, who furrows his brow in thought. This is getting tricky. The good thing is, our competition is a human ship, and Catalan, too. The bad thing, it's a whole cruiser, not a mere corvette or even a frigate like the *Gaudí*.

If things escalate to an armed confrontation (hopefully not), we obviously won't stand a chance against the *Servet* and its capacity of forty-eight thousand tons. Even though it's one of the oldest ships in the Nu Barsa fleet, as a hyperjump cruiser it'll have thirty to forty crew members and, worse, much more powerful, longer-range weapons than our light frigate does.

And if the extragalactics evolved in an aquatic environment, I can't think of anyone better than Nerys to make Contact with them.

"Our guys are in orbit around the second planet in the system, which has roughly the same dimensions as Earth . . . and two satellites, smaller than the moon," Amaya continues, interpreting the data from her instruments. "It has an oxygen atmosphere, water vapor clouds, and . . . " She gulps. "There's another object in the same orbit, a few dozen kilometers away. It isn't sending out any identification beacons. I can't tell if it's a ship or a natural formation. I'm going to visual."

The hologram that pops up in front of us clearly shows the profile—small, because of the distance—of the *Servet*, an ungainly T shape. A hyperjump cruiser doesn't need to have an aerodynamic hull. It can carry enough auxiliary vehicles on board that it'll never have to risk entry into any planet's atmosphere.

But we aren't looking at the large Catalan ship; we've seen it before. We only have eyes for what's in the foreground: a sort of whitish cloud, fluctuating and vague, that makes spots dance before your eyes whenever you try to focus on it.

It definitely can't be a natural formation. A cloud moving through space? But it doesn't look like any ship we've ever seen, either.

We stand there, stunned, jaws dropped, paralyzed, for a very long couple of seconds.

And then we start jumping around, shouting and whistling. We hug each other. Amaya kisses me on the mouth. Gisela kisses Captain Berenguer. Pau and Rómulo hug as if to break each other's ribs. Nuria recites what I think is an Our Father in Catalan. Manu recites something that sounds like poetry, also in Catalan.

For sure. We found the extragalactics!

Who cares if we got here second, if we're in the right place at the right time? The guys in front don't have too big a lead if the guys in back run fast and catch up, as we used to say in Rubble

City. Maybe the *Servet* got here first, but if the extragalactics don't have an aquatic environment we might still have a shot. And if not, better a small share of glory than none at all, right?

"What are the dimensions of that . . . thing?" Captain Berenguer asks, trying to sound indifferent.

"Dimensions, right. Just a sec." Equally excited, Amaya stops, checks her magic sensors, then clicks her tongue with incredulity. "They vary: from two to four kilometers long. Form isn't stable, either; it shifts like an amoeba. Its energy emissions are beyond strange. And the weirdest thing is, according to the gravimeter, its mass and density vary, and some very odd perturbations are showing up on the hypergraph. Which, by the way, I notice is losing power so fast, I doubt it will keep working for more than another few minutes."

"Pure energy? Bioship?" the captain asks, thinking that brevity will hide his excitement.

Amaya, always so certain, again hesitates. "I'm not sure. It's pretty much transparent to my sensors. I'd bet it's made of matter, but these cyclical energy variations . . . I'd say they're metabolic, judging by the biometer readings. It might be . . . breathing."

"Breathing, in space? A living being? That size?" I almost choke, thinking of the Continentines, whole cubic kilometers of cytoplasm. But even they needed a ship in order to venture into deep space. And they couldn't breathe in the interplanetary vacuum.

"I don't know. Maybe. But I'm guessing it has other life forms, more solid ones, inside," Amaya ventures, frustrated by the evident uselessness of most of her instruments. "Exactly twenty-four of them, slowly changing positions. They're four or five meters long. But the thing that's holding or encasing them, the ship or whatever, distorts everything, so I can't be any more precise about the details."

"It might be a bioship fluctuating between hyperspace and normal space," Nuria hypothesizes thoughtfully. "A supercell. And those could be its nuclei, you know?"

Amaya gives her a furious look and opens her mouth . . .

If I let them go on one second longer, we'll have to sit through yet another sterile argument between the former lovers, so I intervene. "We can settle all that later, but for now, why don't we communicate with the *Servet* and see if they already made Contact? Isn't that what really matters?"

"I have a transmission coming in from them now," Amaya notes, suddenly and thankfully busy at the controls again. "I accept and copy."

The holographic image of Alberto Saudat, the old captain of the equally antiquated hyperjump cruiser from Nu Barsa, immediately appears over our heads.

" . . . to the hyperjump frigate *Antoni Gaudí*," says his mono-tone voice, as if he's repeated the same phrase a hundred times already. Then, realizing that he now has a connection, his tone changes to what can only be called one of terrified bewilderment. "Captain Berenguer, condomnaut Valdés! How lucky you're the ones who got here! We need your help urgently. We've located the extragalactics, as you must have deduced from the proximity of their ship to ours. But there were . . . unexpected problems.

We haven't been able to make Contact with them, Nerys is in shock, and . . . "

I'm sorry about what happened to you, my dear slippery mermaid. I think you bit off more than you could chew. Or they made you bite it off.

I don't know whether to feel angry at you or pity you.

Did you think making Contact with creatures from the Magellanic Cloud would somehow be routine?

The hyperjump cruiser *Miquel Servet* was luckier than we were. They found a Qhigarian worldship just four days into the search in the sector assigned to them, Radiants 3567 and 3568. The Alien Drifters were harvesting water comets in the Oort cloud of Epsilon Piscium, and they were delighted to give them the orbital coordinates of the extragalactics they had made Contact with a few days earlier—in exchange for the secret of cold fusion, which I myself had obtained from the Continentines years ago.

Oh, well. Easy come, easy go. Good to know I wasn't the only one who would have happily sold his own mother to drag the damn coordinates out of the Qhigarians. Seems that Nerys also took Miquel Llul's phrase *at any price* completely seriously.

Good thing only two ships from Nu Barsa made Contact with the Unworthy Pupils, because the third might have had to give them the entire orbital habitat in exchange for the same data.

The *Servet*, already knowing what the extragalactics were after and what route they would take, only needed one more hyperspace jump to catch up to them in this system. I suppose the conglomeration of worldships was just beginning to form in the triple Gamma Hydri system at that moment, or else it would have been a lot harder for them to get here, as it was for us.

Reaching the eagerly sought visitors from beyond the Milky Way wasn't the end of the odyssey, of course; it was just the beginning.

The crew of the *Servet* didn't wait the usual three days for a First Contact, of course; the matter was too urgent. The extragalactics allowed them to approach the orbit of their ship with its wavering outline (it almost gives you a headache to look at it) until they were just a few dozen kilometers apart. The Aliens didn't communicate, attack, flee, or show any sign of hostility, fear, or even recognition.

The Catalan crew then figured they might try to make Contact with them. But just when Nerys was nervously preparing to head out into space wearing her ultraprotect, the hypergraph detected a sudden, massive fluctuation, and the condomnaut mermaid disappeared from the airlock—leaving her suit behind.

At first Captain Alberto Saudat retreated to what he thought was a safe distance, but after three minutes went by and no sign of Nerys, he admits he got so nervous he moved the ship back until it almost touched the damned white cloud. He even fired his disintegrating weapons, to see if there would be any response. Not the most powerful ones on board, of course, and he didn't aim them directly at the extragalactics. Just in case.

In any event, my mermaid rematerialized exactly where she had disappeared, six minutes after the event. And in a state of total shock.

"She hasn't recovered," the stunned captain tells us in barely a whisper. "She breathes, she moves, the automedic says she has no neural damage or other internal injuries, but she hasn't regained consciousness. Looks like a regular psychic trauma. Fernando, my life support tech, studied psychology and he's afraid she must have gotten such a huge shock from seeing the creatures, she simply refuses to return to a reality where abominations like them exist."

Wow, great theory for making every other Contact Specialist avoid coming within a parsec of the migraine-inducing cloud ship.

"We tried returning to Nu Barsa to ask for help, but we believe that the hyperengine stops working in the vicinity of these creatures," Saudat continues to whine.

Of course, assuming they did try, it could just be that all the Qhigarians anywhere near here were already gathering over at Lambda Trianguli and not helping out with the hyperjumps; their minds were literally elsewhere. But this isn't the time to tell him that the Galactic Community is about to be deprived of any means of faster-than-light travel—at least until something new turns up.

"And the worst part is, none of the holocameras and other systems on her suit recorded anything. Lucía, my sensor tech, says that was probably because of the same burst of energy that caused the sudden fluctuation we saw in the hypergraph. So we still don't have the slightest idea what sort of creatures we're dealing with," the old astronaut concludes, staring at us.

Or rather, staring specifically at *me*.

Within seconds, the entire crew of the *Gaudí* is staring, too.

All of them except Jordi, the absent third official, that is.

Okay, I get it. I'm the only condomnaut in the neighborhood. Plus, Nerys is my girlfriend.

Succeeding where she failed is now almost a matter of honor for me. That's what they think, anyway.

Captain Berenguer clears his throat and says, nice and slow, "Josué, do you think, maybe . . . "

"Sure." I sigh and shrug, as if to play it down. Though I'm already feeling the first pre-Contact jitters and cold sweats. I still think I make myself sound pretty convincing when I say, "Nerys can be too impressionable sometimes. I should know! I'm going to go put on my suit. In five minutes I can be making Contact with . . . "

"Hyperjump, incoming!" Amaya exclaims at that very instant, ruining the dramatic climax of my speech. Then, voice trembling, she adds, "Human ship, approaching full throttle. I'm checking the radio beacon signal . . . " She gulps and looks up at me, her face serious. "Josué, I don't think you have five minutes to get your suit on. It's ours, too. The *Salvador Dalí*, no less."

Shit. One damn thing after another. I thought the racing-against-time stage of this ordeal was over, but now I'm up against the nanoborg and his vengeful sidekick.

My only consolation is that things couldn't get any worse.

"Incoming transmission," the sensor tech continues, and a hologram appears in our midst.

A day full of surprises for the Nu Barsa fleet, it seems. It isn't Yotuel's tan face, or Jürgen Schmodt's clear blue eyes, or any of the unfamiliar officers and crew members of the *Dalí*. It's an all-too-familiar face, with a jutting jaw and roundly muscular face, looking at us for a moment, grinding his teeth, and at last speaking with an ominous calm: "Last person you wanted to see, right? Perfect. Best if you and the *Servet* back away from the extragalactic ship right now, if you don't want us to disintegrate you. Damned traitors!"

Turns out, things *could* get worse. We're being insulted from the bridge of the Dalí by none other than Jordi Barceló.

"Hold up a sec, Josué, you're almost half a klick ahead of them. You're all three supposed to touch the extragalactic ship at the same time," Captain Berenguer reminds me, his face looking worried in the small holoimage projected inside my helmet. This time he didn't want to delegate the responsibility of being my remote Contact operator to anyone else. "We don't want the crew of the *Dalí* to freak out and start the First Catalan Interstellar War right here, do we?"

"But what if that's what *we* want?" Yotuel smiles venomously from another holographic window.

"*Krieg* if you *mogeln,*" comes the hoarse voice of Jürgen Schmodt, once again looking the part of the model gray-eyed Aryan in a third small holoimage next to that of his protégé.

What's the point of having translation software with thousands of Alien languages programmed into it if he's going to refuse to use it even to express himself in halfway passable Spanish?

My own German translator tells me that *Krieg* means "war" and *mogeln* is "cheat." Clear enough. They trust me as much as I trust them. I never expected any different. No reason to.

This simultaneous triple hololink only proves how complicated the situation has become.

Could have been worse, though. If ours had been the only other Catalan ship in the system, then Jürgen, Yotuel, and especially Jordi Barceló (did the Qhigarians take the DNA sample from his pristine heterosexual rectum instead of his mouth, just to piss off the resentful prick even more?) would definitely have talked Captain Rubén Molinet of the *Dalí* into opening fire on us. Faced with the superior weaponry of the largest and most modern hyperjump cruiser in the Nu Barsa fleet, we wouldn't have had any choice but to flee. Using our inertial engines, to make matters worse, because the hypergraph went dead only minutes after they arrived—meaning that Qhigarian-style hyperjumping has now stopped working throughout the galaxy.

We'll never get out of this system if we don't obtain a new form of faster-than-light transportation from the still unseen extragalactics in the cloud ship.

Luckily for us, Captain Saudat and his *Servet* were already here. Any hyperjump cruiser, no matter how outdated, is a factor to be taken into account in an armed conflict. Maybe the *Dalí* could have dealt with them and us both at the same time—but it would have sustained significant damage in the space battle. So the situation was basically a stalemate.

The three-ship problem, instead of the three-body problem. Everybody frozen, watching the others.

Nobody making Contact, nobody letting the other guy make Contact.

Too awkward to last, right?

The *Dalí* trio started hurling insults and then threats our way. Jordi expanded on all the things he'd do to Amaya and me when he got his mitts on us. Yotuel told anyone who would listen about my more embarrassing childhood adventures in Rubble City. And Jürgen? I never imagined the German would have such a fertile yet rotten sexual imagination. Some of the things he said he'd do to Nerys when he had her at his mercy would make even the most experienced Contact Specialists, like my friend Narcís, blush.

But the bullying phase didn't last long. Once they saw that they couldn't intimidate Berenguer or Saudat into giving ground, they bit their tongues and let the grown-ups negotiate.

Discussions dragged on for three hours, constantly interrupted by "sincere" protests of innocence and marked by open mutual mistrust, but at last we more or less came to an agreement on a joint plan.

That's why the three condomnauts still capable of making Contact are approaching the extragalactic ship at the same time, like good buddies. This way we'll supposedly each get a fair chance. And may the best at Contacting win, right?

Lovely. Such fair play. Brings a tear to my eye.

If this had happened in Rubble City, my sarcastic mentor Diosdado would have said something like, "I want a clean fight—but everything goes."

Two against one. The odds obviously are with the *Dalí* and their two Contact Specialists, first and fourth generation. Hard to say which of the pair is sneakier or hates me more.

I suppose one will try to knock me out of circulation while the other takes his own sweet time making Contact.

A good thing condomnaut suits are designed so you can't carry any sophisticated weapons. Even having a laser telemeter on you is a bad idea: a particularly paranoid Alien might mistake it for some kind of gun, you know. I'd better keep my guard up anyway. They can always try strangling me or breaking my back between the two of them. And it'd be easy enough to hide a shiv in one of the pockets.

I had to accept the risk, of course. Time stands still for no one, and if the extragalactics decide to take off from this system and leave us behind here—I don't even want to think about how embarrassing that would be. Or what consequences might result.

If Nerys had at least come out of shock it would have evened things up a little. Then I'd feel sure that Captain Saudat would support the *Gaudí* with all his ship's arms, to protect his own condomnaut. Oh, well. If dogs had wheels, they'd be carriages. My mermaid still hasn't shown any signs of consciousness. Quite a trauma. . . .

But you can't lose a battle before you fight it, and having the odds on your side doesn't mean you've already won. Point is: sure, it's two against one, but I'm still in the game, still playing.

Sure, I sound as trite as a college football coach or a drill sergeant. It's a pile of clichés, but they work. Even when I use them on myself. It's the magic of motivational speaking.

Now we can see each other. There's no confusing us: Jürgen is wearing a red suit, Yotuel is in white (what a surprise, right?), and they're approaching in close formation from the same direction. My suit is green, as always. I wish it was blue; then we'd be wearing the three colors of my country's flag. So symbolic.

Blood and purity against green, which is the color of hope. And the old flag of Libya, with no other details. How lovely. How allegorical. How full of shit my thoughts get at a time like this. Like I care at all about Gaddafi. Or flags.

"Just five more klicks to the extragalactic ship," Captain Berenguer tells me after checking his telemeter, like mine's not working. "Synchronize your trajectories, though I doubt they'll let you approach much closer. Captain Saudat thinks that at any moment they might telepor—"

Said and done. His voice cuts off, and the next instant we aren't surrounded by the black of space but a softly luminous white. We've been teleported.

It was so soft and painless that, if their hyperengine functions anywhere near as well, I can think of one good reason why the Qhigarians were in a hurry to leave: the Qhigarian mental con game is no match for this system.

We're inside an empty terminal half a kilometer in diameter, according to my sensors. Our comms are cut, of course. The unsullied white of the whole place must make Yotuel feel right at home, as obsessed with cleanliness as he is. I can barely make out his suit: it's the exact same shade.

The air around us is perfectly breathable, and the pressure is correct. Well, a little low, to tell the truth. And—huh. Helium instead of nitrogen. We'll be squeaking like a bunch of Donald Ducks when we try to talk. That'll make it hard to sound like serious ambassadors.

The weird thing is, we're still floating. Don't these visitors use gravity control?

We're still arranged as before: a few dozen meters apart from each other, Yotuel in the middle, me on the right, Jürgen to the left. My two rivals look at each other, make an almost imperceptible signal, and promptly remove their helmets in perfect synchrony.

The empty helmets float like abandoned satellites, while their owners briefly activate the inertial micromotors on the suits and come at me, with the coordinated decisiveness of football line-backers in a slow-motion replay: colorful monochrome uniforms bearing down inexorably on the quarterback from the other team who's got the ball . . .

I was expecting this. Lucky I didn't end up between the two of them. Fighting isn't my thing; I prefer "Here is where he turned and ran" to "Here is where he died." But hey, if you're not going to give me a choice, let's play ball, guys.

I remove my helmet, too (if there are extragalactic bacteria or viruses that our reinforced immune systems can't deal with, we'll figure that out later), and hold it between my hands. Not tight against my chest, like a football player trying to break through the defense and score a touchdown, but slightly away from my body, at eye level, like a basketball player about to shoot a free throw.

I was never any good at football. Standing barely five foot seven and 145 pounds, I wasn't beefy enough, though I'm a fast runner. But I've got a good jump, so I was a better than average basketball player; almost a champion. And now I'm planning to show off some of my skills to this pair.

The helmet is made of light but very hard material. And I was always pretty good at making baskets. A little luck and, first guy that gets near me, I might just break his nose. No, I'd better strategize this. It doesn't matter who's in the lead; I'll go after Yotuel. Jürgen's nanos are made for shifting his body shape, but they also help him to heal disconcertingly fast.

It really is too bad there's no gravity. When I throw the helmet, I'll logically go flying in the opposite direction. For every action there's an equal and opposite reaction: it's the law. Plus, it won't hit him with the classic 9.8 meters per second squared of acceleration force it would have on Earth.

But speak of the devil . . . The gravimeter tells me we've got microgravity now. We're all settling gently to the floor, which is as white as the walls. It has the soft, strange (and a slightly repulsive, I might add) consistency of jam or gelatin. Luckily it isn't sticky, though.

I flex my legs and keep my grip on my helmet, waiting as the gravity slowly increases, bit by bit. The helmets that my two adversaries tossed aside hit the floor and bounce a little. Jürgen's red helmet rolls almost to my feet. Perfect. If I grab it in time, a second projectile will give me even more opportunities. Why would they throw away such obvious weapons?

Maybe because they're sure they'll easily beat me without them.

My suspicions are confirmed as soon as their feet touch the gelatinous flooring and they continue advancing on me. Their long, weightless leaps remind me of the old recordings Abel showed me one time, about the first humans to land on the moon, in the middle of the twentieth century, on the Apollo 11.

And, yes, I'm a fan of old-time astronauts. I was bound to have some sort of shortcoming, right? Nostalgia for the olden days. I hope Nu Barsa will forgive me. There are worse flaws, after all, even for a condomnaut.

Jürgen pulls a long, thin chain from a compartment in his suit, unwinds it, and holds it up before him with both hands, a meter apart, in the classic pose of a strangler.

A mistake, I think. He could have hurt me more easily and from farther away if he'd used it as a lash.

Yotuel, for his part, is more traditional or orthodox about evildoing. He's gone for a large screwdriver. Good for stabbing, good for slashing: pure Rubble City style. I've got to keep my eye on both of them. In my triple-armored suit, the only part of my head that's really vulnerable to a stabbing by my old pal is my eyes, but if I let myself get distracted by protecting them, the nanoborg could easily take advantage, sneak up from behind, wrap the chain around my neck, and strangle me.

Maybe I shouldn't have taken off the helmet. Too late now; no time to put it back on.

Speaking of which, I can feel its weight in my hands now. The gravity keeps getting stronger. I don't need the gravimeter; my bones and muscles tell me it's almost up to Earth level. Hopefully it won't rise much beyond Earth gravity.

Here they come, running with all their might, white and red. A killer Polish flag against the flag of Libya. Nice image, or colorful at least.

Damn, like I care about flags. Is the air getting to me? Muddling my brain? I've seen stranger things happen.

Let's test it, just to be sure.

Self-examination. What color was the flag of Kiribati?

No idea. That's good: I'm still the same old Josué. And I've got more important things to worry about.

Yotuel will get to me first—and with that screwdriver in his hand, he's also going to find it harder to block or dodge a helmet missile than Jürgen will with the chain.

"Fuckin' bastard!" screams Yamil's little brother, the aspiring murderer, as he pounces with his deadly weapon raised high. I can't help noticing how ridiculous his high-pitched nasal war cry sounds in this helium atmosphere. Revenge of Duckman?

I keep my cool. I've been waiting years for this. . . .

When he's two meters away, I hurl the helmet straight at his face with all my might. It does no good: my hard, green helmet travels all of one meter and stops cold, suspended in midair, as if held by an invisible barrier.

Same thing with Yotuel's huge screwdriver, when he tries to drive it into me with all the force of the years he's spent dreaming of vengeance. A second later Jürgen is caught in the same barrier when he lunges for my throat with the chain.

They both struggle to free their improvised weapons, but they can't get them loose. Seeing this, I don't even try to recover my helmet, which remains stuck in midair. Instead, I calmly walk over to Jürgen's and pick it up (no problem). Good thing the ultraprotects we condomnauts use are all a universal model. Maybe a red-green combo only looks good on parrots, but better safe than sorry. I won't survive long in outer space in a suit without a helmet.

My would-be executioners in red and white are still struggling in vain. They've given up on their weapons; now they're just trying to get at me with their bare hands. First they jump as high as they can, then one stands on the other's shoulders; they're trying to see how high the transparent but invulnerable barrier goes. Now they're running away from me in both directions, trying to find a way around it. But no doing: not only is the wall invisible and solid, it seems to divide the entire terminal in two, from side to side.

I'm intrigued by its nature. My instruments detect no force field or electromagnetic waves. But here it is, impregnable, though my stubborn enemies refuse to admit it.

Having nothing else to do, I sit on the floor, holding the red helmet in my lap. It appears that I'm completely safe from my colleagues and their uncharitable intentions for the time being. All I have to do is wait for our extragalactic hosts to take the next step toward making Contact. They are obviously in complete control of the situation. They've been controlling it from the beginning.

I clear my mind. This is what the ancient Greeks called *ataraxia*, philosophical calm, a state of robust waiting, not mere laziness. Narcís Puigcorbé would be proud if he could see me.

I don't have to wait long. A rasping, whispery sound comes from behind Jürgen and Yotuel. They stop their fruitless efforts to break through the barrier separating us and spin round to face whatever it was that made the curious noise.

An aperture has appeared in the white wall, some two hundred meters behind them according to the telemeter in my suit. Not a laser telemeter, of course. As condomnauts, we don't carry anything that could be mistaken for a weapon.

It's just like Amaya said. The invisible barrier threw me for a moment, but this is clearly another bioship. Maybe I should specialize in races that do biotech when I get out of this. . . .

Lady luck is *loca*. You never know who she's going to smile on. Apparently they're going to start on Jürgen and Yotuel's side. I guess I should appreciate the biblical justice—last shall be first and all that jazz—but damned if I find it funny.

The aperture must be about ten meters across. The weird thing is, I don't see anything coming out of it, but my rival-colleagues obviously do. And they seem not to like what they see.

I pay close attention. Indentations appear at certain points in the strange white gelatinous floor. Footsteps. From them I deduce that the newly arrived invisible creature has four, or maybe six or even eight, feet. Considering that there's about two meters between the right legs and the left, I figure it's about that wide by about . . . five to ten meters long. Big, but I've seen bigger. Not so much to write home about after you've made Contact with Continentines and Kigran rorquals. That's some comfort.

But Yotuel falls at once to his knees and begins vomiting, weeping, wailing, moaning for his dead brother, crying for help from his *babalawo*. Diosdado! Poor kid. He'd probably also be calling for his mother if he'd ever known her. No way he's going to try and take off his suit or make any effort at Contact. He's literally dying of revulsion and fear.

What is it he sees that has him so horror-stricken? Sure, he's new at this, but he must have a lot of experience. Otherwise Jürgen would never have taken him on.

The German Contact Specialist, meanwhile, shows more presence of mind, though he's also trembling like a leaf. The damn professional. Training shows. He manages to get his red suit off. Under it, his skin looks like it's boiling.

His nano-impregnated body is modifying itself before my eyes, trying to adopt the morphology of . . . of what? Damned if I even want to know. It's so weird, watching a First Contact between humanity and a creature I can't even see but my colleagues obviously can. I suppose the barrier between us must also have some curious optical properties. The notion of privacy that this race from another galaxy has is a bit odd, to say the least.

The rhythm of raspy whispers quickens, then suddenly switches to an inarticulate hooting that rises and falls in tone in a suspiciously familiar pattern. I check the translation software: yep, we're in luck. It's the dialect of one of the other six hundred plus Qhigarian worldships that humanity contacted before the Unworthy Pupils fled the galaxy. We're lucky that the extragalactics made Contact with them before us. Also that these creatures learned their language so quickly.

Unfortunately, our invisible visitor's message comes through the translation with typically screwed-up syntax.

"Hello, humans-you. Peroptids-we. Extragalactics-we. No-distant we. Magellan Cloud-Large name-you home-we. Come here-now, no-wish war-you we. Danger-war-other species-power-very, fear-flee we. Seek no-enemies we, distant-here-now, Milk Road name you. Contact Qhigarians-before. Species no-war they. No-weapons they. Flee-distant they. Contact no-useful-very they. No-enemies, yes-war, join you-we? Proceed sex-Contact, tradition-you pact-seal, you-we, now-here?"

Quite the speech. For a First Contact with extragalactics, it couldn't be clearer:

They already know we're humans. Must be the free advertising the Qhigarians gave us. They are the Peroptids (or something like that; maybe it's a Qhigarian term with no precise translation in any human language—peripheral eyes, maybe?) who come from beyond the galaxy, but not from far away, just from the Milky Way's dwarf satellite galaxy, which we call the Large Magellanic Cloud.

They come in peace, fleeing another race that is threatening them, I think, with war. They fear their enemies and are looking for allies (I'm guessing) in the Milky Way. But they need warlike allies; the Qhigarians, who don't fight and have no weapons, can't help them. Makes sense. And they propose making Contact with us, following our customs, if we want to seal the pact and become their allies.

And if Jürgen Schmodt pulls it off, I might as well go back to Rubble City in exile and hide in the deepest hole I can find, because this Nazi will practically be a god in Nu Barsa and throughout the Human Sphere.

Extragalactics with working hyperengines that don't depend on Qhigarian teleportation, looking for warlike allies? My Peroptid brothers, who cares what you look like? If it's war you want, you've come to the right species. Nobody better than humans in the whole Galactic Community. I smell alliance and trade.

The nanoborg can obviously see the Peroptid, and he's doing his best to imitate it. Exactly what fourth-gen condomnauts are good at.

Forced to sit idly by, I watch his swift metamorphosis with envy. He molds his nanoassisted flesh to his will, like clay in the hands of a skilled potter. At least it's giving me a secondhand idea of what a Peroptid looks like.

There are two extra pairs of legs rapidly growing from his sides, just below the ribcage. Still rudimentary, but in a couple more minutes at most I guess they'll be functional. Just as I thought, but eight legs, not six: the longest pair in front, because from the way he's doubling over, the back half of his torso is going to be sticking up almost perpendicular to the floor. You might call this creature a centaur but with six pairs of horse legs, in addition to the pair of super-long arms on its human torso that it also uses in walking. What a weird anatomy!

The long, thick legs have three joints; the front limbs may even have four—they aren't well-defined yet, but I'd say the original model must have segmented insectoid limbs. Six legs or eight, who's counting? It might be something like a mantis, with long raptor limbs in front that can also be folded up and used for walking. Must be that; Jürgen's back is becoming covered in what might well be elytra, the hardened topwings that certain insects possess. If they have wings underneath, they can't be functional; the creature is far too large for flight. But I'd guess they . . . ah. The head is more defined now. Couldn't be any more insect-like than that. A pronotum to protect the back of the thorax; long antennae . . . These nanos are amazing. I'm dying of envy. The things you can do with a couple of hair follicles—it looks like magic. Can't I get me a set?

The head is relatively small, but the eyes are large. The nanos aren't really magical; the real Peroptid probably has faceted composite eyes—that would make sense—but for Jürgen to make himself a similar pair he'd have to change his visual neurology too radically, so he just makes them larger and shifts them to the sides of his head. That's it: Peroptid, peripheral vision. His nose is reduced to the minimum, two orifices. His chin sharpens. There are pedipalps on either side of the face—definitely insectoid—with mandibles opening horizontally, not vertically. Well, at least the German bastard isn't going to have it easy. This is so infuriating, seeing the big prize and watching it get away . . .

Then, all of a sudden, the unthinkable happens. The human mimesis of an arthropod from another galaxy is shaken by an inarticulate cry of horror and in the next moment melts, blurs, dissolves, until in a matter of ten seconds what was once a fairly attractive Nordic male and later a surprisingly faithful imitation of an Alien insectoid has been reduced to a pulsating mass of formless flesh.

The tension was too much. Jürgen couldn't control his own nanos. Like too many Contact Specialists of his generation, the result is that he has turned into a quivering aggregate of cells, only barely differentiated into organs and tissues.

He's fucked and well fucked. I suppose that in Nu Barsa, given enough time, appropriate therapy, hypnotic treatments, nano reprogramming, and other sorts of high-tech black magic, they may be able to return him to a halfway human form. But he won't be able to trust another nanocontrolled metamorphosis ever again. His life as a condomnaut is over and done with.

Deserved it, the bastard. But now what?

The invisible insectoid monster from beyond our galaxy approaches the pile of flesh that so recently was Jürgen Schmodt, seems to analyze it briefly, then turns toward weepy Yotuel—who lets the creature nowhere near him, jumping up and running away screaming in sheer panic until he almost embeds himself in a wall more than a hundred meters away, white suit blending with white walls.

He's also out of the picture for good. Just me left. I stand up decisively and approach.

Yes, it's true. The guys in front don't have too big a lead if the guys in back run fast and make Contact. Or at least try.

The footprints of the invisible Peroptid show that it's turning to face me.

I've made Contact with insectoids before, a couple of times. There's no shortage of such species in the Galactic Community. This won't be as good as my tête-à-tête with the Evita Entity, needless to say, but it's not like I'm weeping buckets over it, either. Though I'm still worried about the panic that put Jürgen and Yotuel out of action. What's so horrifying about this creature that both professional condomnauts found its presence unbearable?

I hold my arms prudently in front of me as I walk, until I touch the barrier—which is still invisible, but no longer solid; it's more like a liquid now. After hesitating briefly, knowing that as soon as I cross through I'll see the Peroptid, I cross it in a single long stride.

Then I see it. And smell it. Shangó, Obbatalá, and La Virgen del Cobre.

All I can do is laugh.

With its small head, composite eyes, long antennae, its anterior thorax perpendicular to the floor, freely swinging its long front legs as it sways on its three posterior pairs of legs, which it keeps firmly planted on the whitish gelatinous floor, the feared Peroptid turns out to be sort of an octopod hybrid: half praying mantis, half cockroach.

Except it's nearly five meters tall and ten meters long. And also—stupid me, I should have guessed it from the colorless interior!—it completely lacks pigmentation. Through its translucent exoskeleton I can see its moving muscles, its digestive system, its lungs. . . .

And its scent is sweet, penetrating, and musky. Quite the monster, isn't it?

I continue laughing and leave the undifferentiated pile of flesh that once was Jürgen Schmodt behind me.

God does exist, or the gods, or the orishas, and they love me.

What irony! For poor Yotuel, just seeing it was too much. (A childhood trauma? Did some client try to threaten to throw him to the cockroaches if he talked about what they did to him?) For me, this being from the Large Magellanic Cloud is completely, comfortingly familiar. It's so conveniently reminiscent of Atevi, my albino *Periplaneta americana mutantis*, champion racer of my childhood in Rubble City, that the very next second, while I continue to move forward, I'm already pulling off my green suit and uncovering one of the hardest erections I've had for a Contact in some time.

Not counting the Evita Entity, of course.

I'm a little worried about certain features of insects' sexual anatomy that I recall. Earth insects, of course; this creature from another galaxy might look very similar to an insect externally, but it's not necessarily the same at all. After all, it has eight legs. Given its size, it also must breathe with lungs, not tracheal tubes, and it's got to have an endoskeleton in addition to its exoskeleton to support its weight.

But the exobiologists will sort all that out later. For now, I'm more interested in knowing if it's a male with some sort of corneous genitalia that I'll have to allow inside my body—depending on the size and texture of the organ, that could be a bit painful—or a female that I'm supposed to get inside. In that case it could be a relatively easy job, if it's got a cloaca like it should, or a very complicated one if, as in certain species of bedbugs, it has no sexual orifice at all and the male has to jab its copulatory organ until it manages to perforate the chitinous exoskeleton and spill its sperm.

But that's all mere details. I haven't come all this way at such a cost to let trifles such as those stop me. If I need a little lube or a chisel, I'll use them. Amaya and the automedic can patch me up later on. It'll have been worth it. Can't make an omelet without breaking a few eggs, eh?

Reacting to my advance, when I'm a few meters away the enormous, translucent Peroptid pivots gracefully and lifts its elytra, braces its front legs against the floor, then opens its back legs wide. An unmistakable invitation. A wet orifice opens before my eyes; I'm one lucky guy, that's for sure. A female, with a well-lubricated cloaca.

"Humans yes-war, allies yes-Peroptids," I begin to say, and the corresponding raspy whispers emerge from my translator.

"Interested Peroptid engine long-range," I continue, while thinking: no matter how much it lowers its rump, I'm going to have to stand on a helmet to reach it.

Good thing I still have Jürgen's with me.

"Welcome to the Clifford Simak Geosynchronic Transit Station," the flight attendant announces in the syncopated sing-song of a pro accustomed to dealing with travelers and tourists. "Anyone wishing to descend to the planet may do so from the shuttle port. Shuttles leave every quarter of an hour. Those wishing to take advantage of the offerings at our duty-free shops, please speak to our uniformed staff. And to all our passengers, we suggest that you take some time to enjoy the exceptional views of Earth on our panoramic holoscreens."

Which of course turn on at this precise moment, to spectacular effect. Murmurs of admiration, applause. We humans are still not used to living in space. It always gives you that little flutter in your chest to see your home planet in all its glory from near-Earth orbit.

I even feel it. Really. And I tear up a little. Sheesh.

The unmistakable disk of cloud-veiled blue grabs all the passengers' attention. Well, almost all. Some would rather stare at me, and I'm not surprised. After making Contact with the extragalactic Peroptid I became the hero of Nu Barsa, of the

Catalans, and of all humanity. My face was on the holonews so often that, even after cropping off my hair and growing out the thin beard I wear now, I could still never hope to pass completely unnoticed in a crowd.

I miss my dreadlocks. But lots of things have changed over the past six months.

The hyperjump cruisers *Miquel Servet* and *Salvador Dalí* and the frigate *Antoni Gaudí* returned with all their crews to Nu Barsa two days after making Contact with the Peroptids. Our new pigment-free insectoid allies from the Greater Magellanic Cloud accommodated all three human ships inside their gelatinous hyperspace vehicle and made the jump to the Catalan enclave in a single bound. Like it was our mother ship—or our taxi, as my ironic friend Narcís put it.

Their hyperjump system turns out not to be all that different from the one those Qhigarian con artists used, after all. It's also based on teleportation and uses living matter: their white jelly-like cloud ships are nothing but Peroptid larvae whose development is modified so that their bodies remain partially outside our three-dimensional space. Or something like that.

Simple and effective, right? For those who understand it, I mean. Count me out. Maybe my friend Jaume Verdaguer (for the record, I finally did get a statue of him put up while he's alive, in honor of his sniffing out the true nature of Qhigarian hyperjumping; a hero's perks) and his handful of crazy physicist buddies understand it, but as for me and most people . . .

Anyway, the point is, it *works*. That's good enough for me. For me and for the rest of humanity.

Hyperspace travel was apparently used in the Greater Magellanic Cloud even before fully intelligent life forms evolved. This discovery has astounded and fascinated exobiologists, both human and Alien. It's hard to understand how a species of creatures similar to our ants could spread across the cosmos without the benefit of intelligence. And to think that nobody believed that the Unworthy Pupils could have evolved out in space. Times sure do change.

Humans in general had to work pretty hard to get over their initial instinctive repugnance to working with gigantic albino octopod cockroaches, but now we get along great with our Peroptid friends. It does help that they can make themselves invisible at will. But we're getting their technology now, and they are also more than satisfied. They wanted allies and they got them.

We Contact Specialists, human and otherwise, have been quite busy lately. Negotiations to turn the peaceful Galactic Community into the Pangalactic Defense Force weren't exactly easy. It's a laborious chore to get thousands of species on the same page about any issue. But the fact that humans and Peroptids worked together to restore communications—after the widespread panic that broke out when the Qhigarians left and their fake "Taraplin" hyperengines stopped working—helped convince thousands of Alien species about the good intentions of our alliance.

To be sure, there's a lot of irony wrapped up in the whole affair.

It took me a couple of weeks to get it. The thing is, if the Taraplins never existed—if their hyperengines were a fraud, just a front that the Qhigarians used to conceal their interstellar teleportation abilities—then now that the whole setup has been uncovered, what sense does it make for us to keep performing the "ancient and sacred" Protocol for Contact?

Especially considering that the Unworthy Pupils probably established the custom millions of years ago as a surreptitious way to gather DNA from the sentient species they discovered. Maybe they wanted to use it to build races of clone slaves, or maybe to enrich their own DNA and create the huge variety they now have in outward form. Either way, DNA-gathering was the whole point. But when the brilliant, paranoid Algolese invented the Countdown device to guard against unauthorized use of DNA taken from Contact Specialists, the system stopped working for the Alien Drifters. It only kept going out of sheer inertia.

So now we just do it because it's the custom? So I let that slimy octopus Valaurgh-Alesh-23 play at being my otorhinolaryngologist and proctologist just because "habits are hard to break"? And then I "slept with" the supersized Peroptid version of Atevi for the same reason? And that's why all the condomnauts of the Galactic Community do it?

I doubt it. But nobody's even dared to bring the subject up. I suppose it's hard for any rational being, human or Alien, to admit that we've been acting like idiots for such a long time. We already had to accept that we were taken in by their so-called hyperengines; it might be too much to ask of us to admit that the Protocol was another con.

Or else, there's lots of us who actually like having an excuse for a little sexual experimenting.

The fact of the matter is that, even without Taraplins and Qhigarians, it looks like our Protocol for Contacts and our condomnauts will be around for the foreseeable future.

I just hope nobody gets the bright idea of trying to make Contact with the Peroptids' enemies.

We still haven't learned much about those mysterious extra-galactic invaders, so powerful and cruel that the Peroptids fled the Greater Magellanic Cloud in search of allies to fight them. The Peroptids don't even have a name for them. In their culture, naming something means recognizing that it exists. They think that defeating an enemy starts with rejecting its reality.

At the moment, the best guess is that they come from beyond the Milky Way and its dwarf satellite galaxies, though their ultimate origin is far from clear. As for what they're like, our allies—who aren't very skilled yet at making themselves clear; or perhaps, as our strategists suggest, they're elusive about revealing valuable military secrets—say that they are creatures from negative space.

What's that supposed to mean? Antimatter? We'll have to make them clear that up for us. Just in case.

The bottom line is, they utterly ruin everything they come across, more interested in destruction than in conquest.

I just hope they find our friends the Qhigarians on one of their conquests and wipe them out.

Actually, our new allies think the Unworthy Pupils took off in such a peculiar rush simply because they feared the ruthless creatures. They must have come to the terrifying conclusion that, after finishing with both Magellanic Clouds, the unnamed enemies would come after our galaxy next. Being pacifists, which in their case means cowards, they opted for putting some distance between themselves and the new threat. Just as I figured. After all, if another species was going to take away their monopoly on hyperspace travel, why stick around?

Maybe we'll meet up with the Qhigarians again someday, now that the metagalaxy has been opened up by the living Peroptid ships, with their capacity for long-range hyperspace travel. If we do, we can hold them accountable for their cowardice and their centuries of scamming us all. And find out why they did it.

Meanwhile, several human exploratory ships with Peroptid hyperjump (bio)tech have visited far distant galaxies. And in the Whirlpool Galaxy, the third planet of one red giant has been named—guess what? Josué Valdés! And it's being terraformed to become New Catalonia.

I have the honor of being the First Citizen of the brand-new colony, the first colony established by humanity beyond the Milky Way. And I expect it won't be the last.

Someday I'll visit it, I suppose. If the Peroptids don't abandon us to our fate and deprive us of our hyperjumping capacity, that is.

But not right now. Because today I start my vacation, and have I ever earned it. The special circumstances that make for smooth Contact between human and Peroptid condomnauts have forced me to work hard, without a break, for weeks and weeks.

I feel aches in muscles I never knew I had. Female Peroptids can be very demanding. In their species, males are not sentient beings, so ever since the females discovered the allure of "sleeping with" their intellectual equals they won't leave us alone, day or night. By "us" I mean the few Contact Specialists who aren't overcome by disgust at the thought of giving them what they want.

My good friend Narcís tried to console me once by saying he figured the albino cockroaches must find our bodies every bit as repulsive as we find theirs. Well, guess what—he was the second human to make Contact with a Peroptid. He came out of retirement to do it. Didn't want to miss the party, I guess. So I'll let him believe whatever he wants, if it makes him and Sonya happy.

My relationship with Nerys ended abruptly when the mermaid finally came out of shock, after two weeks of therapy. She didn't want to see me anymore, not even by holoscreen. She sent me word that a man like me, a man so dirty he'd agree to have Contact with creatures as repulsive as those bugs, had better not come anywhere near her, ever again.

Not very professional of her, was it? Well, I heard she's going to leave the Department, to Miquel Llul's dismay.

Jordi Barceló never revealed what it was the Qhigarians did to him, but he also left the fleet. I heard he's trying to get back into the Navy. Better for him, and for Gisela and Amaya, who almost came with me on this trip. But he left Antares in the *Gaudí*. Lucky them!

Jürgen Schmodt still isn't exactly himself. He's back to looking almost 50 percent anthropomorphic, but he still gets the occasional spasm of chaotic dedifferentiation. I dropped in to visit him before I boarded the hypership to Earth and he didn't recognize me, poor guy.

Yotuel did, though. He started howling incoherently, saying I was a cockroach disguised as a human and demanding insecticide so he could kill me and prove it. The psychiatrists aren't very hopeful they can cure him, but I donated a few million credits for them to give it a try.

I don't hold grudges, and Diosdado wouldn't have liked to see me being hard on one of his other kids.

I'm closer to Earth now than I've been in eight years. And I really am feeling emotional.

Sonya, Narcís's wife, asked me before I left if I felt like an exile coming home in triumph.

I'm not sure. I don't feel like a winner, but the truth is, I haven't done too bad.

I decided to go into exile, and I got real lucky. That's all.

But I always felt something was missing, and after years of living in denial, I think I've finally screwed up my courage to admit to myself what it is—and to come back and find it.

"Josué Valdés," a voice comes over the speakers. "Please come to the main lounge."

It's time. I swallow hard and start walking, leaving the hypnotic panorama of Earth behind.

I once left this planet promising I'd never return. I willingly gave up my childhood, my origins, everything that made me myself—for what?

Well, you can't keep all your promises, can you? Especially not the promises you make to yourself.

It took years, I had to cross half the galaxy and make Contact with dozens of creatures born under other suns, but I finally figured out for myself something that Diosdado always told us, the moral at the end of one of his *patakíes*, his orisha fables: it isn't truly a journey unless it ends right back where it started.

Though a place can never be the same as the one we left behind. Just as we can't be our same selves, either. You can't really go back: that's the true secret behind nostalgia.

But sometimes we find more than acceptable substitutes. And every return is a new departure.

Lucky for me, Abel agreed to meet me here in the Station this first time back. Neutral ground. Meeting him down there, on Earth, in CH, in Rubble City, would have been too rough for me.

I just hope he doesn't laugh when I give him back the thousand CUCs he loaned me eight years ago. When friendship has been interrupted, it takes a bit of ritual to mend it. Repaying a debt is as good a ritual as anything.

JUNE 22, 2009

ABOUT THE AUTHOR

YOSS (José Miguel Sánchez Gómez). Havana, Cuba, 1969. Stature: 170 cm. Weight: 75 kg. Right-handed. Atheist. Doesn't enjoy eating avocadoes or cucumbers. Teetotaler. Doesn't drink coffee, and doesn't smoke either. Likes spicy food. Biologist, black belt, and an aficionado of pumping iron, speleology, and military history. Dances salsa, merengue, and rock´n´roll. Hates reggaeton. Prefers rock and classical music. Plays the harmonica. Has been the lead singer of a heavy metal band, Tenaz, since 2008. Full-time novelist, essayist, columnist, humorist, raconteur of scientific facts, and chronicler of realist, sci-fi, and fantasy narratives. Considered the foremost Cuban author and one of the leading Latin American authors of these latter two genres. Has published over 30 works, and his writing has appeared in nearly a dozen anthologies.

ABOUT THE TRANSLATOR

When he isn't translating, DAVID FRYE teaches Latin American culture and society at the University of Michigan. Translations include *The First New Chronicle and Good Government* by Felipe Guamán Poma de Ayala (Peru, 1615); *The Mangy Parrot* by José Joaquín Fernandez de Lizardi (Mexico, 1816), for which he received a National Endowment for the Arts Fellowship; *Writing across Cultures: Narrative Transculturation in Latin America* by Ángel Rama (Uruguay, 1982), and several Cuban and Spanish novels and poems, including *A Planet for Rent* and *Super Extra Grande* by Yoss, both published by Restless Books.